STRIKE
FORCE
7

Ian MacAlister

A FAWCETT GOLD MEDAL BOOK

Fawcett Publications, Inc., Greenwich, Connecticut

STRIKE FORCE 7

All characters in this book are fictitious, and any resemblance to persons living or dead is purely coincidental.

For Commendatore Joachim Burmeister
and the Villa Romana in Florence,
where much of this book was written.

A small slim girl in jeans and a loose dungaree shirt came out of the arched doorway from the courtyard. Diana, the Bishops' seventeen-year-old daughter. She looked toward the parking lot with a puzzled expression on her pert, freckled face.

Then she saw the gun in Bel Zaara's hand. She suddenly became very still, expression and color drained from her face.

Bel Zaara motioned with the .45 and spoke in excellent English: "Turn around and walk in front of me into the house, Miss Bishop."

Diana Bishop just went on staring blankly at the gun in his hand, too frozen to respond. She seemed somehow to become smaller and younger; and very fragile.

Bel Zaara motioned impatiently with the .45 again. "Please do what I tell you."

Inside the villa, a woman screamed in horror.

ONE

The window near the ceiling was still as dark as the rest of Jarrell's cell when they came to take the Tunisian to his appointment with the guillotine.

It was a very small window, opening into a cramped side corner off a courtyard confined by high walls. Daylight wouldn't reach it until almost eight in the morning.

The condemned cells were in another part of Les Baumettes, the maximum security prison of Marseilles. The news was rapped through the wall to Jarrell by a convict in the cell on his left, after having been code-relayed down between the other sections of the Baumettes. It took time. Jarrell estimated precisely how much time. By now the condemned man would have already taken off his faded prison outfit, and put on his own clothes. A sensible government economy. Prison blues were the tax-paid property of France, could be used by other convicts for years to come, and bloodstains were hard to wash out.

Jarrell didn't have to feel around in the dark to find his tin cup. He knew where each item was. And he didn't have to get off the thin, lumpy mattress. The cell was small enough for everything to be within reach. Sitting up, he passed the message through to the cell on his right, by tapping the cup against the wall.

When finished, he put the cup back down in exactly the same place. He raised his knees, braced his hands on them, and leaned his shoulders against the cold stone of the wall. And began waiting.

He was wide awake. His nerves tried to tense up on him, but relaxed under a practiced application of control. Knowing *how* to wait was something Jarrell had learned long ago. It was a necessary tool, to restrain the high-strung tension that was an ingrained part of him.

He was a tall man, built lean and hard, with a strong-boned face that a checkered past had left its marks on. The stubborn humor of his mouth was belied by alert, quietly watchful eyes, making him hard to read.

Taking his right hand from his knee, Jarrell got a cigarette out of the pack tucked between the mattress and the wall, and stuck it in a corner of his mouth. Then he put his hand back on his knee. He didn't light the cigarette—not yet. His eyes were watching the utter darkness in his cell while his mind followed the doomed man through the ritualized steps to execution.

By now the rituals inside the condemned cell were over. Priest, public prosecutor, and the murderer's own attorney had all said the same thing in different words: begging him to show courage during his last minutes of life. The steel manacles had been removed from his wrists and ankles.

A final glass of rum.

The last cigarette.

The step from his cell into the outside corridor.

The executioner waited for him there. With two hefty assistants. The murderer belonged to them now. They took him along the corridor and down the stairs, holding each arm tightly.

In his own cell Jarrell heard, through the still invisible window near the ceiling, a creaking sound out in the prison courtyard. That was the guillotine, being raised into position.

Jarrell slid the tip of his tongue across the end of his unlit cigarette and concentrated on the bitter tobacco taste.

Down inside a room leading to the courtyard, the executioner used a large pair of shears to scissor away the condemned man's shirt collar. His wrists were tied tightly behind him. The door was opened.

After that it always went very quickly. The condemned man was led or dragged into the still murky courtyard. The guillotine loomed before him, with its thirty-eight pounds of honed, slant-bladed steel poised at the top, glinting in the dawn light.

The stronger of the executioner's assistants hit the condemned man in the stomach, low and hard. He fell on his knees on the rocking cradle of the guillotine platform, his torso sagging forward. On the other side of the guillotine, the executioner grabbed his ears and tugged his head down, so the neck fitted into the groove.

The releasing mechanism snapped open. The heavy blade dropped and thudded home into the groove. The sound was audible through every cell window facing the courtyard.

Jarrell lit his cigarette.

In 1097, Bohemond maneuvered his knights like well-drilled fighting machines outside Antioch, smashing Kerboga's larger army of Turks at the Iron Bridge. Jarrell considered the two main mistakes responsible for Kerboga's defeat. First, setting up his main camp too close to the battle area, so that his Turks were forced to stand and defend it, instead of continuing the hit-and-run skirmishing they were so good at. Second, allowing Bohemond to get all his forces across the river, instead of striking while the Crusader army was split in the process of crossing.

Jarrell began analyzing alternative tactics that could have won Kerboga a victory over the Crusaders that day.

His cell window showed gray as morning light finally penetrated that corner of the prison courtyard outside. Some of the light reflected into his cell. Jarrell went on working his way through the strategy of the First Crusade.

Three years they'd sentenced him to. At this point he'd served almost half of it. Spending much of each day like this; methodically rethinking battles he'd studied in the low-intensity operations courses at the Warminster School of Infantry in Wiltshire. It was as good a way as any of keeping his head together in here, so he could walk out still reasonably in one piece.

He rarely thought of home. That was Canada, and Canada was a long way back. Something he'd put behind him; like the marriage that had sunk without a trace, and a wiped-out career as an officer in the British Army. That was another side of him that experience had reinforced: cutting off from pasts that hadn't worked out.

"Leave the dead," the commando survival code put it, "and just keep on going."

Jarrell was thirty-six, and still doing exactly that.

He considered, with a kind of bleak-humored clarity, what it all had added up to: He was a man with a great deal of experience, and very little to show for it. The SAS commando training, the antiguerrilla experience in Cyprus and Kenya, and the resigned captain's commission had gotten him those contracts training native troops in North Africa. The profits from that, and his knowledge of weapons, had gotten him a nice little arms-dealing company. And *that* had gotten him the three-year stretch in Les Baumettes.

It had been a legitimate business, in partnership with a Corsican ex-mobster named Marcel Venturi. The trouble had started with various secret services not approving of some of the parties they sold arms to. Licenses required for legal buying and selling of weapons and ammunition began to be denied. By stubbornly continuing to operate in spite of that, Jarrell had automatically changed from a legitimate dealer into a gunrunner.

He'd been trying an illegal run out of Toulon with a boatload of Brownings, 3.5 bazookas, and ammo when the French customs patrol had showed. Confiscation of cargo and boat had wiped out the company, and every franc he and Venturi had invested in it. Venturi had already flown ahead to Oran to get the buyers ready on the receiving end; otherwise he'd have wound up with the same three-year stretch.

One and a half years Jarrell had served of that sentence. Now he sat there in the claustrophobic confines of his cell, winning battles lost long ago—while he waited to put Les Baumettes with the other parts of his life that he'd left behind.

The greased slide and clank of the double bolts on the other side of his cell door brought Jarrell to his feet in a smooth, unhurried movement. A guard, the one with the close-set eyes and fat chin, came in. He dumped Jarrell's street clothes on the mattress.

This day ended it. He was getting out.

The devil knew where Marcel Venturi had gotten the kind of bribe money to accomplish that.

The guard glanced at the cell window. "You heard?"

Jarrell nodded, his face impassive.

"He died well, that one." The guard had a faintly puzzled expression. "He refused the rum, and walked the entire distance with his head up. No holding back."

"People can surprise you. Sometimes."

"A degenerate like that—a man who would kill a little girl like that—it is hard to understand."

"Did he spit?"

Underworld romantics claimed that the really tough ones could prove it by getting up enough saliva even when they beheld the guillotine waiting for them.

The guard shook his head. "I don't believe that story. At least, I have never seen it." He shrugged away the possibility, and then gave Jarrell a slightly worried smile. "Well, you are not sorry to leave us, I think."

"Not much."

"Maybe we'll run into each other in a bistro, one of these days, eh? Maybe you will even treat me to a *calva*."

"That's possible."

"You have no reason to hold bad feelings against me?"

"None at all."

True enough. In a year and a half inside this place—which had a reputation for guards ranging from rough to sadistic—not one had mistreated him. Marcel Venturi had passed in the word: He considered Jarrell a member of his family, like a blood relation. From a Corsican, that meant something very specific. The guards didn't live inside the prison. They didn't care to spend all their

11

outside time waiting for that kind of vengeance to catch up with them.

After the guard left, Jarrell took off his prison suit. He folded it neatly on the end of the mattress, and put on the clothes he'd been wearing when he'd entered Les Baumettes. They were a little loose on him now.

Jarrell lit another cigarette and leaned against the wall. Angrily, he shoved away a temptation to consider the tactics of the first battle of Acre. The time for games was over.

He considered, instead, how many years he had left to salvage something from his life. That depended—on how much longer his specialized skills could be expected to stay sharp enough. He didn't like the answer.

He thought about it while he watched the cell door, waiting. And while he waited, the other thing was beginning—hundreds of miles to the south, in Morocco.

The cobra's mouth opened wide in warning, displaying the bright scarlet interior—and the wickedly curved, needle-sharp poison teeth in the corners of its jaws. When no immediate danger presented itself, the mouth closed, becoming once more a barely visible slit. The snake slithered the rest of the way out of the opened basket, the yellow and green scales of its thick length glinting dully in the dimmed sunlight that filtered down to the tree-shaded square of the Xauen *souk*.

Coiling and uncoiling in the dust, the cobra slithered slowly toward the smell of the small creature wriggling inside the tied bag lying in the dry dirt ahead of it.

It stopped as it became aware of other living smells; many of them, far too many. Abruptly, it reared from the dirt, its tail coiling tightly to hold the rest of its swaying length upright. The poised head turned quickly, tiny black eyes scanning the humanity crowded in a circle around it —at a respectful distance. Humanity that stared back with dread and awe at the duality the snake conveyed: the evil powers of darkness, mingled with the divine power of life and death.

One human was not keeping a respectful distance. The

12

cobra's head stopped turning as its eyes fastened on this man. A sibilant hissing sounded from its nostrils. Its hood opened wide, quivering as it displayed the eye designs that hypnotized its fear-sick victims.

A hand shot down and snapped shut around the cobra, just below the head, jerking it into the air. The entire length of the serpent spasmed in rage; coiling tightly around the thin forearm extending from the hand, then uncoiling swiftly and lashing at it again and again. But unable to wriggle from the grasping hand. The livid red mouth opened wide again, showing the deadly curved fangs. But the snake was unable to twist enough to sink them into flesh. The grip of the skinny fingers was too strong.

Holding the struggling cobra aloft, the man turned slowly in the dust of the market's open square, displaying it to his gathered audience. About half were local Arabs, with a few women swathed in the traditional white *haiks* that concealed everything but the eyes. The rest were Berber tribesmen from the surrounding Rif mountains; their women unveiled, with gaily striped cloaks and huge straw hats festooned with plumes and mirrors. All watching with frowning concentration, waiting for the rest of it.

He was naked, except for loin cloth and turban. He was small and scrawny, his face a mass of wrinkles where the stained white beard did not hide it. And he was very dirty. But he was El Hadj Yacoub, who had made the pilgrimage to Mecca and been blessed with power over all venomous creatures, so their poison could not harm him. Or so he claimed—and many believed.

He began chanting softly to the cobra writhing in his right hand, the singsong phrases a mixture of praises to Allah and magical incantations from forbidden cults of reptile worshippers. Reinforcing El Hadj Yacoub's occult power were rings with strange devices which festooned the fingers and thumb of his left hand—in contrast to his right hand, which was naked so as not to hurt the snake it held. Continuing to sing softly to the cobra, El Hadj

Yacoub brought it close to his face, gazing into its malevolent black eyes.

Its head strained forward, an inch from his nose. Unable to close that small gap, the cobra kept flexing its long body in nervous, constant movement, lashing El Hadj Yacoub's bare chest, curling around his right arm, uncoiling and whipping at his neck. The gaping red mouth shut and its stringy tongue shot out, the forked end flicking the man's face, leaving streaks of saliva across his cheeks and nose. Its hissing grew low and hoarse.

Suddenly, El Hadj Yacoub threw the cobra up in the air. His right hand caught it deftly, this time by the very end of its tail. Instantly with the catch, he began spinning around in a circle, very fast, whirling the snake over his head like a length of yellow-green rope. The encircling audience drew back, afraid he would let go. But he did not let go. He spun faster, his bare feet churning up a cloud of dust around him. The cobra, swung out full length by the end of its tail, kept trying to coil and strike, but was prevented by the centrifugal force of the spin. El Hadj Yacoub's chanting grew louder, and ended abruptly in a shriek that called upon all his powers to protect him from the deadliness of the poison.

Just as abruptly, he stopped spinning. Before the cobra could adjust to the change, while it still dangled, twitching, from his hand, he flung it around his neck. There were horrified gasps from the audience. El Hadj Yacoub let go of the snake, extending both arms out wide.

The cobra struck with blinding speed, its curved fangs sinking into the meager flesh of his right shoulder. There was a low sound from the gathering; part sigh and part moan. El Hadj Yacoub betrayed no pain. Instead, an expression of deep contentment spread across his wrinkled, grimy face. He kept his arms outstretched as the snake sinuously unwound from his neck and dangled full length down his chest. For a time he let it hang that way, from the teeth embedded in his shoulder, while his blood trickled down from the puncture wounds.

Then he reached up with his right hand and grasped the cobra delicately, just below the jaws, with thumb and

14

two fingers. A hard squeeze, and the red jaws popped open, the fangs pulling out of the bleeding puncture wounds. He began again the soft chanting that would protect him from the venom now racing through his bloodstream.

Cobra poison acts swiftly, attacking the entire nervous system at once; twisting its victim into a paralyzed knot, squeezing the lungs to a stop until it brings on heart failure. With a small victim, it is all over in seconds. With a victim as large as a man, the approach of death is obvious within a minute. Yet El Hadj Yacoub stood there, turning slowly and smiling peacefully at the encircling faces. Utterly unharmed.

The gathering began cheering wildly, shouting the praises of El Hadj Yacoub's prowess. Yet there were some skeptics among them. He could see their expressions—impressed in spite of themselves, but recalling tales of snake charmers who had cut out the venom sacs at the base of a performing snake's fangs; of other charlatans who let the sacs remain, but milked out all the poison with a spoon just before a performance.

Still smiling and holding the cobra with his right hand, El Hadj Yacoub squatted over the bag lying in the dirt. With his left hand he opened the bag and pulled out a small, squirming field rat. Beside the bag was a cage made of sticks set close together, its lid opened. He dropped the rat into the cage, dumped the cobra in with it, and shut the lid.

The cobra contracted itself into a tight mass of coils. The rat, squeaking hysterically, backed trembling into a corner of the cage. The cobra reared on its coils, swaying slightly, the hood expanding to reveal the terrifying designs, the tiny black eyes coldly evil. Its victim seemed already paralyzed, too locked in fear to even attempt finding a way out of the cage.

The cobra lunged, its scaled length uncoiling in an explosive driving movement as the cowled head darted forward. Its forked tongue retracted as the needle points of the curved venom teeth bit into the cowering rat. For the instant required to inject the poison its teeth remained imbedded. Then the cobra opened its mouth wide and let go, drawing back and watching.

The rat tottered and fell on its side; struggled up and fell again, convulsing as the poison knotted it into a tight, paralyzed ball. It died very quickly.

A shuddering sigh came from the gathered watchers. El Hadj Yacoub looked gravely at the skeptics. The doubting sneers were gone. They had just seen with their own eyes that he was no charlatan. Even after biting him, the cobra had retained enough venom to kill the rat. Yet the poison that had entered his own system had affected him not at all.

Gathering up his striped, homespun *djellabah*, he wrapped its voluminous loose folds around his scrawny figure while coins were thrown into the wicker dish near his feet. Acknowledging the contributions with a dignified nod, El Hadj Yacoub slid his feet into his yellow *babouches* and tied a rope around his waist. From the rope hung a bag, into which he transferred the coins from the wicker dish as the crowd dispersed to its marketing.

The fact that all the coins were very small did not upset him. This was not how he made his living. Snake catching was his profession. Farmers and householders who spotted poisonous snakes around their property sent for a snake catcher to ferret them out and remove them. And there was increasing business from tourist hotels and villas. Performances like this were merely a form of advertising; to spread the fame of El Hadj Yacoub as a man with special powers of communication with serpents, able to find them wherever they hid, and call them forth from their holes. A lucrative business, for a man with a reputation.

El Hadj Yacoub gathered up the wicker basket, the empty bag that had held the rat, the basket in which he had brought the cobra, and the cage holding the snake and dead rat. Leaving the open square, he made his way out of the crowded *souk* and entered narrow, nearly empty streets that became little more than loose-stoned paths climbing to the edge of the town between brown walls gaily washed here and there with light blue. He had enjoyed his short stay in Xauen, so deliciously different from most of Morocco's arid hardness, with its gardens, red-tiled roofs and masses of cool green trees. But there was not enough work to stay longer.

His little panel truck was parked a short way outside the village, in the shade of a wild cedar grove. It was an old and battered vehicle. Snakes were painted on its sides; a cobra on one side, a viper on the other. By these, people plagued by serpents knew of his presence in their neighborhood.

El Hadj Yacoub opened the rear door and dumped what he was carrying inside, including the cage. He was shutting the door when he first became aware of two tall figures standing between the trees on his right, watching him. They were very close, yet they had held themselves so still in the shadows of the trees that he hadn't noticed them until they moved.

They moved again, lazily, one step closer; saying nothing. A thrill of terror ran like ice through El Hadj Yacoub.

Long, curved daggers with silver-decorated hilts hung from their waist ropes. That was not unusual in the Rif hills, where most Berbers carried knives, swords, or even guns somewhere on their person. But these were not stocky Rif Berbers. These men were tall and thin, holding themselves with proud arrogance in their tattered black robes and hoods. Blue-dyed veils hung loose under their chins. Some of the dye had stained their faces.

Lean, sun-darkened faces. The faces of cruel-eyed falcons.

Tauregs. The sinister "blue men" of the Sahara desert. They gazed upon him with cold smiles, enjoying the sick fear that froze him like the rat hypnotized by the cobra.

El Hadj Yacoub tried to speak. But his throat was too constricted for the words to come out.

A cultured voice behind him said quietly: "Turn around, please, Yacoub."

It was only with terrible difficulty that El Hadj Yacoub forced himself to turn slightly away from the black-robed

17

Tauregs. The man standing close on the other side of him looked much like them, though a bit shorter and wider in the shoulders, and dressed in a ragged brown-and-gray-striped *djellabah*. He was about thirty, and held his strong figure with the same erect arrogance as the two black-robed men. But there was a thoughtful intelligence in his hawklike face that went with the cultured way he had spoken.

A man of the Chleuh tribes from the harsh inner passes of the Atlas Mountains to the south, El Hadj Yacoub guessed; close relative to the Tauregs. The Chleuhs and the Tauregs were a different breed of Berber, with vestiges of an eerie religion of cruelty clinging to them from a bloodstained past.

"I am Bel Zaara," the cultured voice said quietly. "You have heard of me."

The fear squeezing El Hadj Yacoub's intestines did not loosen. Everyone in Morocco knew the name. Bel Zaara had been a lawyer, educated in Europe and practicing in Rabat, the Moroccan capital—until the latest failed attempt to unseat the government. Then it had been discovered that Bel Zaara was the leader of a revolutionary movement seeking to unite the efforts of rebel rightists and leftists, in combination with an armed uprising by certain savage tribes of the southern mountains and deserts to which it was rumored Bel Zaara was related. The presence of the two Tauregs seemed to confirm that last rumor.

Uprisings against the governments of Morocco were, of course, as old as Morocco itself. For that reason alone the name of the country—"the land of the last sunset"—was so apt. It was a place where so many people continued to experience their last sunset, in such an incredible variety of ways. A land of shaky governments and periodic blood baths, where the intrigues constantly cooking beneath the surface kept boiling out into the open.

Here, modern Europe came into bizarre contact with an Islam frozen in the Middle Ages. Increasingly, Morocco was a favorite of hippies, tourists, and the international jet set. They had seemed unaware of what was happening around them, until last year's attempt to assassinate the king by shooting down his plane. Most of them remained unaware that the man who had plotted the assassination, the minister of defense, had in the year previous put down another uprising by chopping the hands off two thousand rebellious tribesmen and strangling an opposition leader with his own hands.

He had died for plotting the assassination. So had many others involved in the plot. Thousands more who were suspected of involvement were in prisons. Bel Zaara had escaped, and vanished. There was a reward for anyone who could tell where he was.

El Hadj Yacoub did not feel honored that he was being entrusted with the answer. He sank to his knees, shivering all over as though it had become suddenly very cold.

Bel Zaara did not find it strange for another man to kneel before him. That was part of his breeding and lineage. His smile was benign, but heavy with total authority. Reaching down, he seized El Hadj Yacoub's left hand carefully, and turned it over to expose the inside. One of the many rings on that hand was turned inward. A tiny sharp needle stuck out of its large stone.

Bel Zaara smiled. "I thought that was how you did it."

El Hadj Yacoub remembered him now, among his audience around the market square. He'd been wearing sunglasses then. His expression had been neither credulous nor cynical; merely thoughtful.

"You milk the snake before the performance," Bel Zaara continued lightly, "and pour the venom in the hollow of this ring. Then, for a time, the snake is harmless. All you suffer when he bites you is a little pain, a little bleeding. You pick up the rat with your left hand, and inject the venom from your ring. Fools watch, and do not see; and believe the snake's bite killed it. You are a clever little man, Yacoub."

Delicately, Bel Zaara drew the poison ring from the skinny finger and threw it away into the trees. "It is because you are clever that I know you will not betray me. If you did, these two would visit you one night. Or other men like them."

El Hadj Yacoub couldn't bring himself to look at the

Tauregs. He knew they would be watching him like killer falcons, restrained only by the invisible leash of Bel Zaara's control. Just as he knew the terrible truth of the words Bel Zaara was speaking now: "You only play *at* death, snake charmer. These men play *with* death. It is their only toy."

It is difficult to swallow with no saliva in one's mouth. "Please," El Hadj Yacoub begged in a croaking voice, "what is it you want of me?"

"There is a new villa on the coast near here," Bel Zaara told him in a quiet, reasonable voice. "Near El Jebha. It was built as a winter vacation retreat by an American named Simon Bishop. A very wealthy and important man. He can be most useful to us, even without wishing to be. But he is not there now. His wife and daughter are; waiting for him. I must know when *he* will arrive. To learn this, I need a way to enter the villa for a time, without arousing suspicion. So—you will go there to rid their house of snakes. I will be your extremely stupid assistant."

El Hadj Yacoub's terror had grown with every word. He was being told too much; being trusted with too much dangerous knowledge. "But perhaps . . ." he quavered, ". . . they have had no snakes as yet——"

"Tonight, you will creep close and leave some, for the servants to spot in the morning. A practice not unknown, I believe, among snake catchers."

"But—I am expected at another place tomorrow—the hotel at Kalah Iris."

Bel Zaara placed the tip of one finger on the kneeling man's head. "I wish this of you, Yacoub," he said gently. "You will do this thing for me."

The gentleness made it more terrible. It was the gentleness of someone with a divine right to deprive people of life for his own purposes, exercising that power without anger, pleasure or pity—with no more emotion than one feels plucking a weed from a garden.

El Hadj Yacoub's head bowed lower under the faint weight of the fingertip. "Yes," he whispered, "I will do it. Anything you wish, I swear I will do."

Bel Zaara had expected nothing less. Fear was the great mover. For as long as this man continued to be needed, he would now remain his slave. In Morocco there is a saying: "You must kiss the hand you cannot cut off."

They started down the hills toward Morocco's north coast in the small panel truck.

In that same hour, on the other side of the Mediterranean, Earl Jarrell walked out of the prison gates in the south of France.

TWO

The bar was near the old port in Nice. It was a small place, smelling of strong coffee and pungent wine, with a zinc bar, brightly painted round tables, and an assortment of comfortable old chairs. Marcel's wife, Stella, had bought it with money she'd stolen from her husband's pockets over the years and squirreled away. It was all they had left, from the early days when Marcel had run much of the prostitution in Marseilles, his later time as leader of a highly successful bank holdup gang, and his attempt to go straight in partnership with Jarrell.

Stella got to Jarrell first, as he came in the door. Her blond hair was a dye job now, and there were creases in her firmly plump face; but she still had much the same figure that had made her a money-earner back in the days when Marcel had begun his career as her pimp. They put their arms around each other and she did some happy crying against his chest. Then they both looked toward Marcel Venturi, who stood waiting against the bar, regarding Jarrell with a worried frown.

Short and stocky, at fifty-two Venturi was still a rock-hard man who could frighten other hard men by looking at them a certain way. He was also still darkly handsome, and vain about it, wearing his thick black hair the old-fashioned way: parted in the middle and plastered down with perfumed pomade. He advanced from the bar with the sure, catlike tread Jarrell remembered. His hug bent

Jarrell's ribs. Then he stepped back and studied Jarrell, frowning again.

"I don't look that bad," Jarrell growled.

"You don't look like you just came from a holiday on the beach, either," Marcel stated flatly.

A dockworker came in out of the sunlight. Stella went behind the bar to serve him, drying her eyes with a towel. Venturi led Jarrell to a table where a full bottle of scotch and two large glasses were waiting.

"I'm sorry I wasn't at Les Baumettes to meet you," Venturi apologized as they sat down. "But you understand. Just to see that place, even from the outside, makes a pain in my liver."

When he was a very young hood, Marcel Venturi had spent six unpleasant years in Les Baumettes. He'd been sentenced to sixteen, for wiping out a rival pimp in a knife fight. But the guards had gotten deliberately lax during World War II, and Venturi had been one of the many who'd escaped. Like most of the Corsican mobsters, he'd joined with the Resistance—as a killer of French mobsters who were cooperating with the Gestapo. For murdering some fourteen of them, the authorities after the war had wiped out the rest of his sentence, plus all records of his criminal past.

Which was why, the next time he'd been nailed for a crime, it had to be charged as a first offense. It wasn't knocking over banks that had landed him in court again. It had been a matter of two heroin dealers cutting the throat of a nephew of Venturi's for stealing from them. They'd been expecting Venturi after that, of course, and had been waiting with revolvers in their hands when he walked in carrying a sawed-off shotgun.

That had enabled Venturi's very expensive lawyer to plead self-defense. He'd also pointed out that the death of that particular pair was no loss to French society, and reminded the court of Venturi's heroic war record. As a result, Venturi had drawn only four years that time.

But four plus six added up to ten years of Marcel Venturi's life spent inside the walls of Les Baumettes. Which accounted for his reluctance to get anywhere near the place again, and his attempt to avoid it by going into a legitimate business with Earl Jarrell.

They drank their first toast to freedom, and then Venturi was studying him again, still not smiling. Venturi wasn't much of a smiler. He'd lived in southern France most of his life, but the Corsican dignity and seriousness ran deep in him; along with the bandit savagery.

Jarrell's nostrils pinched as he got a whiff of Venturi's familiar hair pomade. "How much did it cost you to get me out, Marcel?"

Venturi waved the question aside. "Now is not the time. First you have to relax and become used to living again. In a few days I'll give you the bill."

He meant that literally, Jarrell knew. There would be a bill, laboriously hand written, with each expense listed in detail.

Jarrell refilled his glass and drank again, savoring the hot glow. "It had to come high. We were both broke when I went in. Where'd you get that kind of cash?"

Marcel Venturi shrugged his thick shoulders. "There have been a number of jewel robberies along the Riviera in the past year."

Jarrell regarded him soberly. "That's taking quite a risk, for a man who doesn't want another look at Les Baumettes, even from the outside."

"You are my partner," Venturi said simply. "You would have done the same for me."

"I'm not so sure."

"*I* am sure." Venturi watched Jarrell down another double. "Not too much more of that, my friend. You have a girl waiting for you, in a room at the Hotel de Paris in Monte Carlo. A good room, with a view of the sea. And a good girl; exactly what you need."

Jarrell smiled crookedly. "Both part of the bill?"

Venturi didn't see the humor of it. "No. The room and the girl are a present. From me and Stella. To welcome you back."

Jarrell woke the next morning at the accustomed time, just before dawn. But there was no lingering illusion that

24

he was still in his prison cell. He came out of sleep between smooth sheets, wrapped in the naked warmth and softness of the plump little redhead, who had been every bit as good for him as Marcel had promised.

Carefully extricating himself from the girl and the bed, he crossed the thick pile of the carpet to the open window. A cool breeze bathed his skin. He sucked his lungs full of the fresh sea air and looked across the darkness of Monaco harbor. A pale line of light was growing along the horizon.

The girl had helped. Along with the luxury room, an excellent meal, a long hot bath followed by a cold shower, and half a bottle of very good scotch. And then more of the girl.

But Jarrell knew it was going to take a lot more than that to get Les Baumettes out of his system. And still more to make up what it had cost him. From now on, his relaxing would have to take the form of preparation. A week of going through back issues of the newspapers. And then, once he was in the picture, some specific digging around.

Somehow, somewhere, he'd have to find a way to make the money to pay Marcel Venturi back. Along with enough to give his own life a new direction, before middle age landed on his back and slowed him down.

He had no idea, at this moment, how he was going to get that kind of money. But this was a world in which there were always buyers for the kind of experience and skills he had to sell.

Something was bound to come along.

Bel Zaara allowed the snakes to kill El Hadj Yacoub before driving the panel truck down to the Bishop villa for the last time. It was not an act of gratuitous cruelty. It was cruelty with a purpose. It insured that no one would be left behind to reveal what they had done until they and their hostage were safely hidden where the government troops could never find them. Simultaneously, it provided a little amusement to blunt the edge of his Tauregs' boredom.

Nine days had passed since the morning when El Hadj Yacoub had first driven up to the Bishop villa, with Bel Zaara in front beside him and the two "blue men" concealed inside the back of the panel truck. While Bel Zaara stood by looking stupid, El Hadj Yacoub had humbly explained the reason for his visit. He had been driving past on his way to a job at a hotel further along the coast, when he had become aware of the presence of snakes here. Many of them; all poisonous. He proposed to gently remove them, for a modest fee per snake.

Mrs. Bishop, a beautiful woman of about forty, told him graciously that there were no snakes on her property. This was echoed by her daughter. Also by Reagan, their bodyguard, a former member of the American Secret Service employed by Simon Bishop to watch over his family. El Hadj Yacoub assured them they were wrong. The souls of the snakes had communicated with his in passing.

A bit worried by his certainty, Michele Bishop had called the two Moorish servants. But neither of them had seen either of the snakes that had been left close to the house just before dawn.

This was not a problem unknown to El Hadj Yacoub. He proposed a simple solution, to prove both his honesty and his talent: He would search the grounds outside the house for an hour. If nothing was found, he would drive away and there would be no charge. If he did turn up a poisonous snake, he would be paid to find the rest—a small sum for each one caught.

It was too reasonable a proposal for Mrs. Bishop to refuse. For half an hour El Hadj Yacoub wandered around the small estate, smelling and listening, while his stupid assistant followed him carrying an empty basket with a lid. Finally, El Hadj Yacoub began rapping sharply on various rocks with a heavy forked stick. There was a low hissing from a hole under one rock. El Hadj Yacoub deftly extricated a wriggling brown viper with the forked end of his stick, and dumped it in the basket. Bel Zaara closed the lid, carried it to the panel truck, and returned with another empty basket.

Half an hour later El Hadj Yacoub caught the other

snake he'd planted; this one a cobra. After that, he had no trouble getting permission to search the inside of the house.

Thoroughly frightened by then, Mrs. Bishop and her daughter stayed outside on the terrace beside the pool, together with the two servants. But the bodyguard followed El Hadj Yacoub and Bel Zaara from room to room, to make sure they didn't steal anything. Bel Zaara had already given El Hadj Yacoub instructions for such a situation. The snake catcher suddenly began cursing his stupid assistant, for forgetting to bring another empty snake basket after taking the cobra away. Bel Zaara scurried out to the panel truck. The bodyguard, unable to follow them both at the same time, elected to stick with El Hadj Yacoub's house search.

They were off searching through the bedroom wing when Bel Zaara returned to the house through the living-dining wing. It was a matter of only a few seconds for him to take a sophisticated electronic listening device from the snake basket, and attach it behind the back of a Moorish-style desk on which the telephone was set.

Two hours later El Hadj Yacoub announced that there were no more poisonous snakes inside the house. The viper and cobra he'd caught had been the only ones. The villa was once more safe.

Paid the modest amount agreed upon, they drove off —but not far. Just to the top of a cliff behind the villa. There, concealed in a small palm grove, Bel Zaara entered the back of the truck and turned on a sensitive radio receiver and tape recorder tuned in to the electronic bug he'd planted inside the Bishop villa. Both the equipment; and the expertise to use it, Bel Zaara had acquired during a recent visit to Rome. And both had served him well.

Yesterday evening he had finally heard the news he'd been waiting for: Simon Bishop would arrive from America today. His own helicopter and pilot would already be standing by at the Rabat-Salé airport, ready to fly him quickly the rest of the way to the villa.

Bel Zaara thought about Simon Bishop as he maneuvered the panel truck along the dusty dirt road twisting down through the broken cliffs toward the sea. A figure of international importance, this Mr. Bishop. His multitudinous financial empire controlled a varied group of powerful corporations with branches in many countries, including one of the world's biggest airlines. A man of incalculable influence, wealth, and prestige.

And yet, just a man. A man who could be taken, and held—to force the present Moroccan government to give in to certain demands, in exchange for his life.

There was a possibility, Bel Zaara realized, that the government would not believe he had the courage to carry out his threat, with a man of such importance. In that case, the fate of the very important Simon Bishop would teach them to believe him the *next* time. The government would learn a number of surprising lessons about Bel Zaara, by the time he toppled it.

Bel Zaara kept the panel truck in second gear and his foot on the brake as he drove down the steep twists of the road that had been hacked and blasted out of the rugged brown-rock slopes rising from the sea below. Thirty feet above a tiny sand beach, the road leveled off onto a table of flat rock. It was a natural feature, enlarged by engineering. The Bishop villa had been built on one end of this level area. There were no other buildings in sight. Simon Bishop had bought the whole curve of sea cliffs and hills at this point, to insure total privacy.

The half of the level area that was used as a pad for the Bishop helicopter to land and take off had been left bare rock. But grass, and some healthy-looking palms and lemon trees, sprouted from the truckloads of rich soil that had been spread around the area containing the villa. The architecture of the villa itself was a graceful recreation of Moorish-Spanish style: two rambling wings of white and golden-brown walls rising to multilevel flat roofs from which sprouted white-washed domes. One wing was wrapped around a tiled terrace and swimming pool facing the cliff. Contained within the other wing was a courtyard, with a fountain and shade trees, open to the sea. Steps cut in the solid rock led from the courtyard down to the small beach.

The oval parking area was near one windowless side of the villa. A dusty white station wagon and a blue sports car were parked in it when Bel Zaara drove up. Reagan was already leaning against the station wagon, on guard in a relaxed way, when Bel Zaara brought the panel truck to a stop.

Reagan was a bulky, balding man with mean, suspicious eyes like two little blue holes in a sun-reddened face. The loose sports shirt he wore didn't conceal the powerful width of his shoulders or the growing paunch. Or the hard outline of a revolver worn high on his waist in a belt holster. He stepped away from the station wagon and looked curiously at the cab of the panel truck, wondering about El Hadj Yacoub as Bel Zaara climbed down.

"Haven't seen any more snakes," he drawled in a grating voice. His French was so bad it was barely understandable.

Bel Zaara grinned stupidly. "El Hadj Yacoub sends gifts for Madame Bishop." He pulled an open basket of fresh fruit from the front seat of the panel truck, and set it on the ground.

Reagan looked down at the fruit in the basket, frowning.

Bel Zaara got a second open basket from the seat. This one looked empty. He picked it up with his left hand and reached inside it with his right hand as he turned back toward Reagan. "This is from—"

The three words were enough. By then he was facing Reagan. Even with the basket muffling the sound, the noise of the .45 automatic going off inside it was very loud. The heavy slug tore a small hole through the bottom of the basket and punched a larger one in the middle of Reagan's broad chest, slamming him against the side of the station wagon. It left a fist-sized opening coming out of his back, and disintegrated the station wagon's side window and windshield.

Reagan sagged away from the station wagon and fell to his knees on the ground, his balding head sagging. But the revolver from his belt holster was in his hand.

That could only have been pure reflex action. The rest was not: With an enormous effort of dying will power, he tried to bring the gun up.

Bel Zaara drew the .45 out of the basket and blew the back of Reagan's head apart with a second point-blank shot. The bodyguard spread out in the dust and did not move again. Bel Zaara dropped the basket, stepped over the dead man, and moved past the cars toward the villa. On the other side of the villa, his two tribesmen from the south appeared out of the rocks and closed in on the building like swift dark shadows.

A small, slim girl in jeans and a loose dungaree shirt came out of the arched doorway from the courtyard. Diana, the Bishops' seventeen-year-old daughter. She looked toward the parking area with a puzzled expression on her pert, freckled face.

"Reagan, if you're target-practicing again, Mother said—" Then she realized the bodyguard was nowhere in sight. She switched her attention to the advancing Bel Zaara, and shifted to French: "We heard some—"

And then she saw the gun in Bel Zaara's hand. She suddenly became very still, expression and color draining from her face.

Bel Zaara motioned with the .45 and spoke in excellent English: "Turn around and walk in front of me back into the house, Miss Bishop."

The girl just went on staring blankly at the gun in his hand, too frozen to respond. She seemed somehow to become smaller and younger; and very fragile.

Bel Zaara motioned impatiently with the .45 again. "Please do what I tell you."

Inside the villa, a woman screamed in horror.

Diana broke out of her trance. "Mother—?" She spun away from Bel Zaara and ran into the courtyard.

Bel Zaara strode in under the doorway arch after her. It was deliciously cooler inside the court. The dark shadows of the walls and the fruit trees around the tinkling fountain lay across the marble-tiled flooring. Diana was running past the fountain toward the entrance to the living-

room wing of the villa. Her mother came out of it, blocking the way.

"Don't go in there!" she shrieked at her daughter.

Diana stumbled to a halt, staring at her. Michele
Bishop was as small as her daughter, but her figure was
fuller, beautifully curved in the simple, sleeveless white
dress she was wearing. Her face was twisted with a sick
horror that obliterated its loveliness, aging her grotesquely.
She repeated what she had shrieked, this time in a choked
whisper: "Don't go in there . . ."

Abruptly, her legs gave way under her and she sat
down. There were bright-colored cushions piled against
the shaded wall, but Michele Bishop couldn't manage the
single step that would have taken her to them. She sat
down on the marble tiles.

Diana shot Bel Zaara a frightened look and then sat
down beside her, seizing her arm with both hands.
"Mother, for God's sake what's—"

The Tauregs came out of the living-room doorway.
The lean curved knives they carried were bright with
dripping blood. Diana's mouth opened soundlessly and her
eyes went wide. Michele Bishop just stared dully at the
flooring tiles. The Tauregs grinned at Bel Zaara and wiped
the blood from their blades on the cushions. Sliding the
knives back into their scabbards, they drew long-barreled
Luger pistols from inside the ragged folds of their black
cloaks. Holding the Lugers carefully, they squatted down
on either side of the two women, watching them without
expression.

"I'm sorry, Mrs. Bishop," Bel Zaara said softly, "that
it was necessary to kill your servants. But it was for your
sake, and your daughter's. To prevent further bloodshed.
They made too many to watch and control at the same
time. Someone might have made a mistake."

Diana looked up at him, fighting against her fear. "What
do you want? If you came here to steal, you don't have
to kill anybody for that!"

"Please don't insult me," Bel Zaara warned her thinly.
"I am not a thief. This is a political matter." He looked
at Diana's mother. "You have nothing to worry about,

Mrs. Bishop. In a little more than an hour, your husband will arrive here by helicopter. We are going to take him away with us, using the helicopter and its pilot. You and your daughter will be left here, securely tied but not hurt. When we have Simon Bishop safely hidden away, I will make a phone call to the authorities. They will come here and release you—and find a paper listing my demands for your husband's release."

Michele Bishop looked up at him dully. "So that's what it is—a kidnapping."

Bel Zaara shook his head in irritation. "No. Not the kind you mean—for ransom money. It is an act of mercy, Mrs. Bishop. The government of this country is currently holding thousands of men as political prisoners. Nine of them are scheduled to be executed in two weeks. I will release your husband—in exchange for one hundred of these political prisoners whom I will list, including the nine scheduled for execution."

"My husband has no connection with the politics of this country," Michele Bishop said with gathering anger. "You have no right to harm him because of your own—"

"I don't *intend* to harm him," Bel Zaara cut in. "I would have nothing to gain by harming him. He will be released, quite unharmed, when the present government fulfills my demands. It is that simple."

"What if your government *doesn't* give in to your demands?"

"It is not *my* government. It is a collection of stupid, vicious men supporting a king who is destroying my country. But none of them are stupid enough to risk being responsible for the death of an important man like Simon Bishop. They will release the prisoners I designate, in exchange for his life."

There was no point in explaining further to this rich, spoiled foreign woman. She could know nothing of the psychology of this country, where the news of such a daring success would bring hundreds of wild tribes flocking to join the small number he had with him now. And she could know nothing of the dream he dreamed. A dream that had almost been realized some fifty years ago by Abd-el-Krim, the Rif leader who had come very close to sweeping the whole nation under his banner.

Abd-el-Krim had made one mistake. He had rallied thousands of mountain tribes behind him, but had failed to gain the cooperation of the main cities. Where Abd-el-Krim had failed, Bel Zaara would succeed. The hundred political prisoners he would force the government to release included all the dissident city leaders: the extreme right and left, the pan-Arabists, the angry students, the overambitious army factions. They would rally to Bel Zaara's cause when he struck at the cities with the legions he would gather. The dream was a practical one.

He was brought out of it, suddenly, by a noise in the sky, echoing against the cliffs. Frowning, Bel Zaara stepped out from under the shading overhang of the house and looked up.

A helicopter was circling down toward the villa.

Quickly, Bel Zaara stepped back into the concealing shade of the overhang. Simon Bishop could not possibly be arriving this early. The plane bringing him from America wasn't due to land at the Rabat-Salé airport for another half hour. Bel Zaara couldn't understand—and it worried him.

He spoke sharply to the Tauregs, and warned the Bishop women to remain exactly where they were. Striding off alone, he went through an arch-shadowed passageway between the two wings of the villa, climbed three blue, clay-tiled steps, and entered a bedroom. He crossed it swiftly, and looked out the windows toward the flat bare rock of the empty half of the level area.

The helicopter was just touching down in the middle of that open space, its whirling rotor blade churning up thick clouds of yellow dust. It was a big Huey chopper, converted to carry five passengers in comfort. The noise of the motors cut off, and the rotor blades slowed to a stop. As the dust settled, Bel Zaara could see the pilot clearly through the big windows. He could also see that there was no passenger.

Turning away from the window, Bel Zaara went swiftly back to the courtyard. He spoke to the Tauregs, then to

Michele Bishop: "Understand me quickly. Your daughter stays here with my men. You go with me to speak to the pilot before he comes in here. Your husband is not with him. I want to know why he came without him."

Diana almost smiled with relief. "So you're out of luck," she told Bel Zaara nastily.

He didn't bother to glance at her, keeping his eyes on Michele Bishop as she rose to her feet. "You will use your intelligence. If you say anything wrong, my men will kill your daughter. Understand that."

Michele Bishop nodded quickly, her face stiff. "I do understand it."

"Good. Walk ahead of me."

She crossed the courtyard and went out through another of the arched doorways. Bel Zaara followed her closely, holding the .45 out of sight behind his right thigh. They stopped just outside the doorway. The pilot, a stocky former army flier named Dave Baker, was coming toward them from the helicopter, his boots scuffing up dust with each step. He looked upset about something. Whatever it was, it had nothing to do with Bel Zaara, whom he barely spared a curious glance as he reached them.

"Hello, Dave," Michele Bishop said, trying to keep the tightness out of her voice. "Where's my husband?"

Baker took off his peaked fisherman's cap and hesitated, looking at her. "Listen, Mrs. Bishop, first of all I'm supposed to tell you it's nothing to worry about. Nothing at all. Mr. Bishop himself talked to me, half an hour ago. And you got to figure, if he can make long-distance phone calls, he's got to be okay."

This time Michele Bishop didn't try to keep the tightness from her voice: "What is it, Dave? What's happened?"

"Seems like Mr. Bishop, just before he was going to take off on the transatlantic flight, had a mild—I repeat, *mild*—heart attack."

"Oh, my God—"

"I told you, Mrs. Bishop—your husband's *okay*. I mean, I talked to him personally on the phone. Which they sure wouldn't let him do if he wasn't okay. He said to tell you it was a very mild attack. He's only got to stay in the hospital in New York three or four days. No more'n that, he says. And he's already feeling a lot better. Only of course he can't fly over for a while, now. So I'll take you and your daughter out of here to Rabat. You can catch the next plane out to America to be with him, and see for yourself. He says he'll probably already be back on his feet by the time you get there."

Bel Zaara brought the .45 up from behind his leg and put it against the side of Michele Bishop's head. "Put your hands on top of your head," he told Baker, "and turn your back to us."

The pilot stared, stunned.

"Please do whatever he says," Michele Bishop said quickly.

Bel Zaara nodded. "Unless you want your employer's wife killed."

Baker laced his hands together on top of his head and turned away from them, still not quite absorbing it. Bel Zaara patted Baker's pockets and under his arms with his free hand, and found he was not carrying a weapon. "All right, Mrs. Bishop, take him inside and rejoin your daughter."

Baker turned back to them and started to take his hands down from his head. Bel Zaara told him softly: "If you make a false move, *she* dies first for it. Keep that in mind."

Michele Bishop seized Baker's thick wrist and dragged him into the courtyard with her. "It'll be all right soon," she whispered to him. "If we only hold onto our nerve a bit longer—"

Bel Zaara ordered them to sit on the tile floor beside Diana, and be quiet. He stood over them, holding the .45 down beside his leg and thinking it through under the changed circumstances while the Tauregs waited and watched impassively.

Bel Zaara's mind worked with sharp clarity, spurred by necessity. He thought, first, of two men who were waiting for him to return to their mountain stronghold with Simon Bishop. One was his uncle, Allal Ben Hafidi; a tough old

35

warrior who at this moment held together a loose coalition of twelve savage mountain and desert tribes. The other was Colonel Omrani, who with ten under-officers had managed to escape the government's mop-up of military leaders involved in the attempted assassination of the king.

Bel Zaara's only hold on these men lay in accomplishment. If he now returned empty-handed from this mission, the coalition he was forming would come apart.

He did not intend that to happen.

It came to him, quite suddenly, that the changed situation could turn out to his advantage. Holding Simon Bishop as a hostage *would* have been a powerful lever against the Moroccan government. But a Simon Bishop who was free—and thus able to apply all that pressure personally—could be an even more powerful lever.

All that was required, now, was to give Simon Bishop an incentive to apply all that power.

Bel Zaara spoke softly to the two Tauregs.

They rose to their feet, looking down at Michele and Diana with eyes like slits of shiny metal.

THREE

The American came down the steps from the Promenade des Anglais to the beach. Pausing at the bottom, he turned his back on the ornate splendor of the Negresco Hotel, still clinging gracefully to its fairy-tale memories of vacationing royalty ranging from Queen Victoria to the czar of Russia. There had been a time when this gilded past had fascinated the American. But not now. He scanned the beach with an impatient, searching gaze.

He was in his fifties. Lines of anxiety cut deep in his homely, blunt-featured face. His thinning hair was a shade of gray that almost exactly matched the color of his summer-weight business suit. But his short, lean figure had a wiry hardness that most men lost by his age. And his skin had the weathered toughness of a man whose business was done outdoors, rather than behind a desk.

There was a challenging physical and mental sureness, almost a bantam cockiness, in the way he stood there looking over the other people along the beach. Not many were left at this hour. In September the sun over Nice began to lose its warmth by six P.M. The American strolled the beach studying those who remained. Just the men; women didn't interest him at the moment. He stopped when he came to a man lying face down near the water's edge.

The swimming trunks this man wore had a light crust of salt from the sea, but were already dry. Beside his long sprawled figure, an old pair of leather sandals weighted down faded jeans and a black polo shirt. There was a long scar running diagonally down this man's flat-muscled back, from the left shoulder blade to the right side of his waist. It made a ragged white line in the newly acquired tan of the skin.

Jarrell turned his head and looked up at the wiry little American. He'd been asleep; but there was no trace of sleepiness in his eyes.

The American said: "Earl Jarrell?"

Jarrell sat up and nodded, sizing the other man up with quiet calculation. He no longer looked like a man with a year and a half in prison riding him. He looked like a man who had spent this day as he had the past ten: six hours hard climbing in the hills behind the Cote d'Azur, two hours in the Nice library methodically reading back issues of the newspapers, a one-hour swim, and a nap to restore the juices for whatever the evening held.

The American was studying him like an owner of a used-car lot estimating the potential of an automobile offered to him for sale. He seemed to make up his mind about something. "My name's Mal Rosen," he said shortly. "I've got a job for you. It has to be finished in less than two weeks. You get ten thousand dollars for coming in. Twenty thousand if we pull it off. And it starts right now."

Just like that. No trimmings. Jarrell took another, more respectful look at the little American. "Who sent you to me?"

"Marcel Venturi. He'll join us at the Nautique Brasserie, as soon as Stella shows up to take over the bar from him."

The use of "Stella" instead of "Venturi's wife" nudged Jarrell's curiosity. "Known Marcel long?" he asked as he stood up and pulled the jeans on over the dry swimming trunks.

"Since the war. Not any of your wars. World War Two. I was one of a bunch of guys the OSS slipped into this area separately before we invaded the south of France. The idea was for us to organize the French partisan groups to keep the Germans busy away from the beaches.

But most of us were just raw college kids with no qualifications, except that we could speak French. So most of us didn't survive to see the invasion."

"But you did."

Rosen nodded. "Because of Marcel Venturi."

Jarrell thought about that as he got into the polo shirt and sandals. He led the way up off the beach and along the Promenade toward the harbor. "All right. What's the job you want done?"

"I guess you know what happened in Morocco yesterday. A revolutionary named Bel Zaara kidnapped Simon Bishop's wife and stepdaughter—and a pilot who works for Bishop—to exchange for one hundred political prisoners."

"I read about it," Jarrell said. "According to the papers, the girl is Bishop's daughter."

"Stepdaughter," Rosen repeated flatly. There was something in the way he said it that Jarrell couldn't put his finger on. "Another thing you won't read in the papers: The government of Morocco's *not* going to make the exchange. They're not going to say that openly because they don't want Bel Zaara to kill the hostages before the time limit he set. This way they figure their army has a chance to find Bel Zaara first, smash him and take the hostages back."

Jarrell shook his head. "I wouldn't bet on their chances. First, they haven't even been able to find the helicopter they all took off in. Second, the Moroccan army and secret police have been hunting Bel Zaara a long time, without getting in smelling distance. Third, even if they do manage to locate him and close in, the hostages would be dead before they could get to them."

"I know that," Rosen said. "So does Bishop. He's put on a lot of pressure, personally to the Moroccan government, and through the State Department. And the American government's put on all the pressure it can, without being accused of trying to intimidate another country's government, and endangering its already difficult position in the Arab world. But Morocco won't make the deal. Can't afford to. Its government's too shaky right now for them to let loose a hundred rebel leaders and hand Bel Zaara that kind of morale builder."

Jarrell walked on in silence for a moment. "So Bishop figures to buy himself a private little army to slip in there, and try locating Bel Zaara and winkling the hostages away from him."

"That's the size of it. I had a talk with Bishop in the hospital before flying over here. He's given me his power of attorney. Unlimited. I can pay out whatever it costs, to get enough of the right kind of men to go in there with me and do the job."

Jarrell frowned at Rosen. "Go in *with* you?"

"I'm in good shape and I know how to shoot," Rosen grated. "Winters I run a ski resort and summers I spend mostly hunting. The last guy that underrated me was in a Pittsburgh bar. Twice my size and half my age—and bleeding all over the floor when I walked out. So don't *you* underrate me."

Jarrell grinned in spite of himself. "Okay, so you're a tough little man. That doesn't qualify you to run a paramilitary operation."

"I don't figure on *running* it," Rosen snapped. "That's what you're for."

"You don't belong on an expedition like this in *any* capacity," Jarrell told him bluntly. "No matter how much Bishop's paying you. This is strictly a job for professionals. Those OSS days are a long way behind you. Too long."

Rosen was staring straight ahead, chewed by an emotion that he didn't let reach his voice. "Bishop isn't paying me anything," he said quietly. "Michele—his wife —used to be my wife, before we got divorced. Diana is *my* daughter. I'm going."

Jarrell didn't say anything more until they reached the Nautique.

They sat at one of the yellow sidewalk tables under the blue umbrellas on the Quai de la Douane ordering double whiskeys. Jarrell leaned back in his chair and sorted out some thoughts. Heavy traffic crawled past, getting in and out of Nice for the evening. In the gathering dusk, lights were going on in buildings around the long, narrow harbor, reflecting on the oily water.

"I want one thing understood at the start," Jarrell said finally. "If I take this on, it's my show. You're just one of the troops. I make the decisions. You carry them out; without question. I sympathize with your personal stake in this, but once we're in operation I won't let that affect my judgment."

"That's how it has to be," Rosen acknowledged. "But remember, the objective is to get Diana and Michele out alive; along with Baker, the chopper's pilot. And any fighting cuts down the chance of that. Agreed?"

"Absolutely. You want to try *buying* them out, first, is that it?"

"Right. I've got Bishop's letter of credit for one million dollars on a Zurich bank. And the authority to make it out to Bel Zaara. That's one hell of a lot of dough for him to put into his revolution, wouldn't you say?"

Jarrell gazed emptily at a Greek coastal freighter and a Russian lumber ship from Leningrad moored to the dock directly in front of the Nautique. "It's worth trying."

Rosen eyed him shrewdly. "But you don't think he'll go for it."

The waiter brought their drinks. Jarrell took a long swallow of his and waited until they were alone again. "Bel Zaara has sworn to kill his hostages unless the government releases the hundred prisoners he named in the list he left behind. That's the kind of blood ultimatum the tribes he needs behind him understand. He'll lose face with them if he backs off from it for any reason— if those prisoners aren't released and he sells his hostages instead of killing them. Bel Zaara is the kind of man who wants his word to stand for something."

Jarrell finished off his drink with a second long swallow and said: "If Simon Bishop's paying for these, I'd like another."

Rosen motioned to the waiter for refills, and finished off his own drink. He was studying Jarrell and considering something.

"But," Jarrell resumed smoothly, "as I said, it is worth

41

trying. So long as we're prepared to launch the alternative the moment Bel Zaara refuses."

"You sound as though you know Bel Zaara," Rosen said.

"Met him once. He handled the pickup on a load of ammo I sold to his uncle, Ben Hafidi." Jarrell shook his head at the way Rosen perked up at that. "Doesn't mean I know where to find either of them. The pickup was made on the coast. Ben Hafidi moves his fighting men around the High Atlas range. That doesn't tell us much. The Foreign Legion spent twenty years combing those mountains for tribes like Ben Hafidi's. The only way they ever found most of them was by walking into their traps."

The anxiety lines in Rosen's face became more pronounced. "We're going to have to do better than that. Bel Zaara's deadline's down to ten days now. Time'll start running out on us pretty damn fast."

"That," Jarrell agreed quietly, "is a fact."

The waiter came back with fresh drinks. Jarrell had another long swallow and looked at the full orange moon rising into the darkening sky over the crest of Mount Alban. Automatically, he checked his watch. Seven-fifteen. He glanced off to the right. Venus was already up there, above the sea wall that sheltered the entrance to the port.

Mars wouldn't be along for another couple of hours. But it was on its way. By midnight it would dominate the sky.

That only happened one year out of every three. It hadn't happened all the time he'd been in Les Baumettes. But now he was out—and Mars was back.

It seemed, under the circumstances, very appropriate.

Marcel Venturi came out of an alleyway onto the quay and joined them. As he sat down the waiter strode over and pumped his hand vigorously. There was something almost regal in the way Marcel Venturi asked after the health of the waiter's wife, children, and mother, before ordering a whiskey for himself and a meal of fish soup and grilled shrimps for all three of them.

When the waiter went inside, Venturi looked at Jarrell and Rosen. "Well, children," he asked quietly, "do you get along?"

"You said he's the man for the job," Rosen said flatly. "That's what I came to you for. I'm taking your word for it."

"You can. Believe me." Venturi looked to Jarrell. "Who else do we take with us?"

Jarrell just looked at him.

Rosen observed the look and said dryly: "Your friend Jarrell doesn't like the idea of dragging *two* old men along."

Venturi went on looking at Jarrell. Something very Corsican crept into his eyes. "Earl does not think I am too old," he said evenly.

"No," Jarrell admitted. "Not for the fighting. And not for the dying, either. You know we'll have everything going against us down there. Including the Moroccan army and secret police. If we get a lead to Bel Zaara, they're not going to like the notion of our not inviting them along."

"Having the authorities against us is not a new sensation for me," Venturi pointed out. "As you know. And the money is worth it. I can use twenty thousand dollars."

"Sure. If you live."

Venturi shrugged a heavy shoulder. "If not, Stella will have enough to see her through her old age."

Jarrell looked to Rosen. "You know he's doing it because the girl's your daughter."

Rosen nodded. "I do know it. Now, how many more men *do* we need?"

"You and I just agreed on what the objective is. For that you don't need an army. You need a small commando team—with exactly the right men." Jarrell was silent for a bit, thinking. Then he nodded to himself. "The ones I want we can get *in* Morocco. Except for one we'll pick up on the way, in Sicily. If he's available."

Venturi frowned a little. "You're talking about that crazy kid?"

"He may be crazy, but he's got a talent with weapons."

43

"I figured that all the men you'll pick for this team will have that," Rosen put in.

"Not the same," Jarrell told him. "The others'll be more like me—men who know weapons and how to use them, as tools. With Gerd von Kleist, it's art. Like the difference between stonemasons and a sculptor."

Rosen got the picture. "So get him. Whatever he costs."

"He won't cost much. Money's not the point with this boy. The job has to appeal to him. I think he'll like this one."

"You see what I mean," Venturi said to Rosen, without humor. "Crazy. And in more ways than that."

"That still leaves us with our main problem," Rosen said pointedly. "Finding Bel Zaara."

The waiter brought Venturi's drink. Venturi waved him out of hearing distance before speaking. "I can make some enquiries around the Arab quarter here in Nice. Sometimes you can pick up odd bits of information there."

"Most of it unreliable." Jarrell sipped at his drink, something nudging his memory.

"That is true," Venturi admitted. "But what about the contacts you've got *in* Morocco? They're the kind that hear things they wouldn't tell the police."

Jarrell was nodding when it came to him: "I've got better than that," he said softly, and looked at Rosen. "Have you got any influence with Simon Bishop's branch offices over here?"

Rosen nodded. "Bishop sent word to his people. They're to give me anything I want, no questions asked. That's in practically every country in the world—including here, and Morocco."

"That's going to come in handy. And they can start being of use right now. You get on the phone to the top man in Bishop's offices here in France. Tell him to make a call—immediately—to somebody with weight in the European branch of Associated Press. I want to know where Nora Devlin is. And I want her told to give me full confidence and cooperation."

Rosen and Venturi were looking puzzled.

"Nora Devlin," Jarrell explained, "is an A.P. reporter.

Presently *persona non grata* in Morocco. Because five weeks ago she did an interview story from down there, and won't tell where the interview was held, or how she made the contact."

Jarrell finished off his whiskey and put the empty glass down delicately. "The interview was with Bel Zaara."

The taxi made fast work of getting out of Nice to the Côte d'Azur airport. Jarrell arrived at the terminal building with ten minutes to spare before his plane took off. He went inside, carrying everything he was taking with him in a small canvas bag slung over his shoulder, and picked up his ticket for Rome at the Air France counter.

He'd left Venturi and Rosen with a detailed list of things to check out before they flew down to Palermo the next morning. Palermo was a necessary stop for two reasons: Gerd von Kleist, and a wily old smuggler named Guido. Jarrell would join them down there later in the day—after he'd pumped everything she knew out of Nora Devlin.

As he joined the last stragglers preparing to board the Rome plane, Jarrell thought with strict realism about his chances of pulling this operation off. And the men he needed to help him pull it.

They were going to be, he knew, his last army. Win or lose, live or die. His last army. And his last operation. He wanted to do it right.

Leaving the terminal building and walking toward the plane, Jarrell glanced up at the night sky. The strong red glitter of Mars was there now, riding high. The glow of the full moon obliterated all the stars in that half of the sky. Only Mars showed—and Venus.

For a long moment, Jarrell stood still and looked up at the heavenly triumvirate: the orange moon flanked by silver Venus and red Mars. Then he climbed the steps into the jet taking him to Rome and Nora Devlin.

FOUR

Nora Devlin was tall and slim in a loose shirt that had
a couple of buttons missing, and an old pair of dungarees.
Her legs were very long and her hair was dark red. She
had unusually large gray eyes, alive with intelligence
and drive. The stubborn set of her mouth suggested guts
to match. She was about twenty-nine; good-looking by
some standards, not by others. The face was too strong-
boned, and revealed too much nervous tension.

She had a large glass half filled with scotch in her hand
when she opened the door, and she gave it to Jarrell with
an odd little smile as she let him in. There was something
faintly malicious in it that puzzled him. He looked around
while she closed the door. Her apartment was on the third
floor of a house in a narrow street off the top of the Spanish Steps. The living room was big and high ceilinged, with
large windows opening on a small balcony. The room was
cluttered with newspapers, books, and magazines in at
least four different languages, the greatest concentration
of clutter around a small desk holding a portable type-
writer.

Nora Devlin perched herself on the edge of the desk and
gestured at a chair, studying him with that faint edge of
hostility he'd sensed when she'd let him in. He sat down
and looked at the glass in his hand. "This for you, or
me?"

"For you, of course."

Jarrell frowned at the very large amount of scotch in the glass, and then at Nora Devlin. "Somebody's been telling you things about me."

She just smiled that funny little secret smile again. "All I was told was to be here and wait for a man named Earl Jarrell to show up. Well, here I am and here you are. Now, what's it all about?"

There was no hostility in that. Only ingrained professional curiosity.

Jarrell took a drag at the scotch, put the glass aside, and told her what it was about. All of it; not holding anything back. She listened to him with intense interest. He could see her brain ticking away behind those large gray eyes.

When he was finished she said, "Jesus, what a story *that's* going to be—if the government doesn't release those prisoners."

"They won't be released," Jarrell told her harshly. "And it may be a story to you. To me it's Rosen's daughter dead, and Bishop's wife dead, and a chopper pilot dead. And most likely not in a nice clean way. Unless I can get to them first; and get them out."

Nora Devlin held her temper in check. "I've seen a lot of people killed, in a lot of nasty ways. In Vietnam, Africa, the Middle East. And I've written stories about it. Because that's my job. Like your job is killing people, or helping them kill each other. That doesn't mean I don't have normal feelings about it."

Jarrell shrugged a shoulder. "Okay. Point made and taken. Now, *can* you help me find Bel Zaara?"

She gave it some serious thought. "I'm not sure. I can't tell you exactly where I interviewed him. Except it was somewhere in the Atlas mountains; and it took over two days to get there from Marrakesh. I was blindfolded all the way. First in a car; then on foot with somebody holding my arm. Climbing all the way. When they finally took my blindfold off, we were in front of a cave with cliffs all around. No special landmarks I can tell you about."

"Was Allal Ben Hafidi there? His uncle?"

Nora Devlin shook her head. "Just a bunch of pretty savage characters acting as sort of a bodyguard for Bel

47

Zaara. They didn't do anything but stand around looking while he talked to me for about an hour, saying the things you read in my story. About the unending corruption of Moroccan governments—which is true. And how he's going to clean up the mess and give his country some self-respect, the way Quadhafi did with Libya—which may or may not be true."

Jarrell nodded. "The usual slop."

Angry color stained Nora Devlin's strong cheekbones.

Jarrell raised a placating hand. "I mean what he had to say for himself, not the way you wrote it. Your article was good solid stuff."

"That's better," she said sharply. "You can criticize anything else about me you want. But not my work." She drew a tight breath. "Anyway, the trip back to Marrakesh went the same. Blindfolded all the way. I couldn't even tell you the direction."

Jarrell hunched forward, watching her. "How did you make contact with Bel Zaara, in the first place?"

"I didn't. He got in touch with me. I was having a drink on the big square—the Djemaa El Fna. A man came over and asked if I'd like an interview with Bel Zaara. Just like that. I'd seen this man around the square before; every day I'd been there. But he'd never spoken to me or even looked at me, that I know of. He said Bel Zaara knew I was in the country, had read some of my Vietnam and Mideast articles, and did I want to meet him? Of course I said yes. So he took me to a car, and when we were outside the city, he put the blindfold on me. And *that* was the contact. I don't even know the man's name."

"You said you'd seen him around the Djemaa El Fna before. Was he working there, at one of the stands or bistros?"

"No. Just wandering around. Now and then he'd talk with other men who came by—very quiet, furtive stuff."

"You're pretty observant."

She shrugged. "It's my business to be."

"Then you can describe what he looks like."

Nora Devlin shook her head. "Nothing that would mark him out for you to recognize him by. Just a medium-sized, skinny Arabic type, like a thousand others you'll see on that square in any single day."

Jarrell chewed on that in silence, not liking it one bit.

"But *I'll* recognize him," Nora Devlin said quietly, "if I see him again. And I got the feeling that square is his hangout. So—I guess you'd better take me along with you. If you can slip me in with false papers or something. The Moroccan government doesn't like me very much since that interview."

Jarrell just looked at her for a moment. Then he said: "You can already smell a Pulitzer Prize in *this* story. That it?" His voice was sardonic. But it didn't quite conceal the instinctive respect he felt for a true professional, in any field.

Her grin softened her surprisingly; almost made her look vulnerable. "That's it. Why not?"

Jarrell let another moment go by, looking at her gravely. "The way things stand, it's probably my only way to Bel Zaara," he told her quietly. "I need that too badly to say No. And I won't insult you by saying what you already know: how rough it could get for you, going along on something like this."

"If I was afraid of that kind of risk," she pointed out evenly, "I wouldn't do the work I do. I've done some of my best stories out of the middle of hell. Notably out along a road they call 'Bitch Route Thirteen' in Vietnam. You may have heard of it."

Jarrell nodded slowly. "As rough as they come," he agreed. "Okay. It's your story, and your skin. And my need. Have your notebooks and some hiking shoes ready tomorrow morning. Fake papers and slipping you in are no problem. We'll take care of both in Palermo tomorrow night."

He still didn't like it. And there still wasn't any other way. He reached for the glass he'd put aside, then changed his mind and took a long steady look at Nora Devlin. "I have a very strong feeling you know me from someplace. But I can't remember. You'll have to tell me."

"I'm not surprised. You were dead drunk at the time." The faintly hostile note was back. "It was in Katanga. I managed to wangle a flight in, to interview some of the mercenary troops that were keeping the Congo fiasco going. The mercs told me you were in town selling arms, and knew as much about what was going on as anybody. So I went to your hotel. You were wallowing in a big bed with two local whores, one brown and the other yellow. All of you bare-assed. You wanted me to take off my clothes and join in."

Jarrell kept his eyes perfectly steady on her. "Did you?" he asked casually.

She flushed. "What for? You were too drunk to talk. And *if* I'd been interested in anything else, you were very obviously too drunk to do anything about that, either. With one woman, let alone three."

"You really do have a nasty way of putting things, for such a talented girl."

"I'm not a girl, Jarrell. The word is 'woman.' Which does not equate with sexual toy."

Jarrell groaned. "Oh, Christ—another one of those."

"Which means exactly *what?*"

He gave her a bland, polite smile. "Nothing that matters a damn. I still need you to locate Bel Zaara, and you want to cover it for your news syndicate. So we're in business. That's what matters."

When she frowned like that, little worry wrinkles showed around the corners of her eyes. "Am I giving you a hard time? I guess I'm just getting even, for Katanga."

Jarrell raised and lowered a shoulder. His smile became amused, less formal. "So you've got a temper. Nothing wrong with that. Shows spirit."

"Don't con me, Jarrell. I've been conned by an ex-husband who was an expert. He thought my temper was amusing, too. Until he had to live around it."

Jarrell laughed and stood up. "I can see how that might happen. Pick you up in the morning. Around ten. Be ready."

He headed for the door.

Behind him, Nora Devlin asked: "Where are you going?"

He picked up his bag. "To find a hotel for the night."

"It'll be hard, this late. I've got a spare bedroom."

Jarrell turned around and stared at her. Then he smiled, just a trace. "I really have the feeling I don't quite understand you."

That funny grin softened her again. "I am rather complicated. But that needn't worry you. The important thing is, your virginity is safe. As I said, it's a *spare* bedroom. I won't come in and rape you. And you won't come out to rape me. Got the picture?"

He put down the bag. "Got it." He walked back and picked up the glass. "I *think*." He drank the scotch.

The house was in an isolated fold of the harsh Sicilian hills behind Palermo. It was a primitive, century-old, two-room structure built of rough stones dug out of the surrounding slopes. Once a meager farm had surrounded it. But generations ago the rain floods that rushed down from the peaks above had washed away the last of the tillable soil. It had been unoccupied for a long time when Gerd von Kleist had bought and repaired it. The place served as a spartan retreat for the life of a hermit-monk which he led between wars he elected to fight in. There was no phone line, no electricity, no plumbing; and the well in the front yard was the only source of water.

Jarrell got out of his rented Fiat and opened the wooden gate, strolling into the small yard. Gerd von Kleist, stripped down to a pair of undershorts, was whitewashing the stone walls of his dwelling. He was twenty-six years old, with a perfection of body and face that one saw in ancient Greek statues of young athletes. But there was a suggestion of gauntness to him now that Jarrell didn't like. And the finely chiseled beauty of his features was haggard, marred by dark blotches like bruises under the bright blue eyes.

He lowered the brush and looked at his unexpected visitor without surprise or enthusiasm. "Hello, Jarrell. I heard you were in prison."

"You heard right. Let's get in out of the sun, Gerd. And I could use a drink."

"Water is all I can offer you."

51

"I've been known to drink water," Jarrell said wryly. He stepped into the house as Gerd went to the well out front.

The main room was fairly large, with a small stone fireplace. It was obsessively neat and clean, almost bare of furniture. There was a mattress with an army blanket and no sheets in one corner, a small standing closet, a single wooden chair, an old kitchen table. That was all.

The door to the other room was shut. Jarrell had never been in there. A man who had been had told him there was no furniture at all in there. Just three walls covered with photographs of concentration camp victims; and a picture of his father on the fourth wall.

Major Franz von Kleist, after wounds received in battle as an S.S. officer, had been made commandant of an obscure Nazi extermination camp in eastern Austria during the last two years of World War II. A very small cog in the Nazi death machinery. But a very great trauma for Gerd, when he found out about it. For the first nineteen years of his life he'd known little of that past. The only child of his father's second marriage, he had grown up in Egypt, where his father was an advisor to the army. He'd worshiped his father, who had responded by teaching him all the manly arts, including the use of weapons. Gerd had turned out to be a prodigy in that line; he had a natural flair, which he'd later come to regard as the devil's mark upon him.

When he was nineteen, his father made the mistake of sending him to Europe to complete his education. There he learned the truth. He dropped out of school and never returned to Egypt, not even when his father died. For a time he became indistinguishable from the horde of world-wandering hippies, except for his secret burden of guilt. At one point he became a near-alcoholic; at another he experimented with hard drugs. Neither satisfied; both seemed to him an evasion of responsibility for his heritage of guilt.

Finally, he had sensed a certain ironic pleasure in using the talent for violence derived from his evil heritage, to fight against evil. To choose what was worth fighting for—and against. The greater the risk, the most satisfaction. Like a legendary knight, doing penance for a stain of sin that nothing could wash away. Complete with a vow of chastity. He hadn't had a woman since he'd learned the truth of his heritage. None of which made sense to anyone else; but it did to Gerd von Kleist.

Gerd came in the door with a tin cup, which he gave to Jarrell. The well water was deliciously cold, sweet tasting. Jarrell sat down on the single chair. Gerd remained standing. In the shade of the room, his haggardness was pronounced. He looked like a sick angel. Sick in body; sick in his soul. Jarrell looked from Gerd to two items resting in the precise center of the table: a wrist watch, and a raw potato.

"I'm making an experiment," Gerd explained. "In exactly thirty-six minutes I can eat the potato. That's what the inmates of my father's camp got to eat in the last six months. One raw potato a day. I'm interested in what that did to them, in body and mind." His smile was boyish; almost sheepish. But it didn't alter the steely determination in the clear blue eyes. "I don't imagine this shocks you. You already know I am crazy."

"No. Not crazy. Just ridiculous. You're not responsible for things your father did before you were even conceived."

"I disagree. 'The sins of the fathers—even unto the tenth generation.' Remember?"

Jarrell shrugged. "We don't live in an Old Testament world any more."

"I do."

Jarrell grimaced with disgust. "How long have you been conducting this one-potato-a-day experiment?"

"Eleven days. I've got a bit more than six more weeks to go."

Jarrell was relieved. Not long enough, considering Gerd's basic health and youth, for any damage that couldn't be restored by a few good meals. He rose to his feet. "Get your clothes on and close up this place. We're going down to Palermo for a thick rare steak with eggs on it. I've got work for you."

"I can't," Gerd told him flatly. "I've set myself to this experiment. Come see me in six weeks."

"By then you won't be of any use. And it'll be too late, anyway. For this job."

Gerd shook his head. "Sorry."

Jarrell slapped him. A brutal, swinging slap that twisted his head around, spun him against the wall, and dropped him to the floor. Jarrell didn't like doing it. But it was necessary. Punishment and authority, two things Gerd deeply required, were needed to shock him out of his one-track concentration.

Gerd pushed himself to a sitting position on the floor, staring up at Jarrell, one side of his face inflamed by the imprint of the hand. "You are lucky," he said calmly after a moment, "that I have such control over my more unpleasant instincts."

"And if you didn't?" Jarrell demanded thinly. "You never have any weapons around here. Without a weapon, all it would get you is knocked down again." Jarrell resumed his seat on the single chair, hunched forward and rested his elbows on his knees, and pinned Gerd von Kleist's eyes with his own. "Now listen to me carefully, Gerd—"

He told him about the operation, the need for it, and the time limit applying an increasing stranglehold on it. Gerd didn't show much interest in the fate of the chopper pilot. But the plight of Michele Bishop and her daughter got to him. He had a virgin's exaggerated feeling for the fragility of women. Jarrell watched him begin to concentrate on the practical problems involved in an operation of this kind.

"You see why I need you along," Jarrell said. "You get five thousand dollars for it. One of Bishop's attorneys is in Palermo. You can have the money assigned to survivors of your father's concentration camp—considering the size of your chances of coming back alive."

Gerd looked at the whitewash on his hands and arms as he rose to his feet. "I'll wash this off and get dressed."

Jarrell watched him go out to the well. Gerd von Kleist,

54

Marcel Venturi, and Mal Rosen—plus Nora Devlin and Jarrell himself.

His last army now numbered five.

When the Moroccan army patrol reached the isolated ravine deep in the Rif mountains, the smoke from the burning helicopter rose in the still air like a solid black column. On a shelf of rock on the other side of the ravine, a large square of cardboard was held down by a heavy stone. On the cardboard was written in a neat script:

"This, from Bel Zaara—Simon Bishop's wife and daughter are still unharmed. But so far there has been no response concerning my demands. Is it, perhaps, that the criminals who control the government doubt that my threats are the words of a serious man? I leave this token, as proof of my unflinching sincerity."

The proof of his sincerity—and the grisly humor of his followers—lay beside the warning note: the body of Dave Baker, the chopper pilot. His severed hands lay at the ends of his ankles, and his feet were where his hands should have been. His head had been placed between his legs.

FIVE

Guido was seventy years old; a fat, bow-legged Sicilian whose knife-scarred face and red bandana wrapped around his entirely bald skull made him look like a pirate out of a bygone era. But the smuggling boat he ran out of Palermo, crewed by his tough-looking son and even tougher grandson, was as up-to-date as they come: a converted PT, the interior revamped for greater cargo capacity and the twin engines restored to their original power.

With a boat like that, Guido had made fast work of the crossing to Morocco. It was still dark when they sighted the *lamparo* fishermen doing their night's trawling out of Al Hoceima. Jarrell stood spraddle-legged on the open flying bridge and scanned the little fishing boats scattered across the flat, black waters, each with its strong acetylene lamp to attract schools of fish to its nets, to be hauled in while the creatures were temporarily blinded by the glare. Beyond the night fleet loomed the long dark bulk of the Rif hills rising out of the surf.

Beside Jarrell, Guido spoke softly to his grandson at the helm. The boy spun the wheel delicately. The PT turned westward, following a course parallel to the Moroccan coast. Soon they could make out some lights in the tight, cliff-cupped bay of Al Hoceima: a few from the little harbor itself, more from the Quemado Hotel off on the beach and the Hotel Mohammed V up on top of the cliff.

Guido signaled to his son in the engine room. The PT slowed to a cruising crawl, still parallel to the coast. Near enough for the pickup boat to come out and find them; far enough for a speedy dash back into international waters if anything official-looking came their way.

Jarrell glanced at his wrist watch. "In ten or fifteen minutes," he told Guido.

"I hope he's dependable," Guido growled. "I don't want to hang around here longer than that."

"This one's dependable," Jarrell reassured him, and went down into the shadowy wheelhouse.

Venturi and Rosen were there, squinting at the coast through the side window. On the floor between them, wrapped in a canvas knapsack with a protective cork lining, was a small battery-powered radio-telegraph transmitter, complete with power pack, transmission key, and wind-up antenna. That might be their most important weapon, when it came to the finish.

The Bishop representative in Palermo hadn't liked carrying out orders he didn't understand; but the orders had Simon Bishop behind them, and he was *going* to carry them out. By now he'd have already flown into Rabat. By late tomorrow there should be radio receivers set up in at least four different spots inside Morocco, tuned to receive signals from this transmitter. Ready to pass them on to one of three helicopters stationed outside the borders waiting to pop in and fly them out in any of three different directions. It could turn out to be that tight at the end; if the operation succeeded in getting that far.

Jarrell asked where Gerd von Kleist and Nora Devlin were.

"Down below," Marcel Venturi told him. "He's telling her the story of his short life. And his father's too-long life."

"She's some interviewer, that girl." Rosen still sounded bemused from his own experience with her.

"If she hears you call her a girl," Jarrell drawled, "she'll chew your ears off."

57

"Already did. And to hell with it. A girl's still a girl by me. Being a talented bitch doesn't change that."

Jarrell went down the steel ladder to the main cabin. They were sitting across the table from each other; Nora Devlin scribbling rapidly in a small green notebook as Gerd told her earnestly: "You should look it up. It was in the east of Austria. It's there in the records, all of it."

"Chalker'll be along in ten minutes," Jarrell told Gerd. And then, to Nora Devlin: "Don't use Gerd's real name. He may want to work this country another time. If there is another time."

"I *want* her to use my real name," Gerd said firmly. "And my father's. Nobody remembers about him. People should be reminded. It's not something that should be forgotten."

Jarrell was too keyed up for a philosophical discussion at that moment. "Ten minutes," he snapped. "Be ready on deck." He left the cabin, going outside to the port deck and squinting shoreward.

The lights of Al Hoceima were out of sight now; cut off behind the high, rocky point that sheltered the bay. There was only the dark, ragged-topped length of coast. And still nothing coming their way. Jarrell looked at his watch again. When he looked up, Nora Devlin was standing there in the darkness near him.

"That's one strange boy in there," she said quietly, a bit troubled.

" 'Strange' is one word for it," Jarrell agreed dryly.

"You're all strange, each in a different way." She said it half to herself; Jarrell could sense her already sorting them out in her mind, characters for a series of newspaper pieces she already saw headlined all over the world. With her byline on them. Nothing wrong in that. Just a professional using special skills and training to achieve the profession's objective.

She went on in the same thoughtful tone: "An ex-gangster from Corsica . . . and you don't have to tell me; I won't use *his* real name . . . and a tough little man trying like hell not to show how he's being eaten up by fright about his wife and daughter——"

58

"The daughter, sure," Jarrell cut in. "I doubt Rosen's that cut up about the other one. She's *not* his wife, remember. Left him for a tycoon who could give her the better things of life."

"That's how much you know. Rosen left *her*—for a younger woman. Quite a number of them, matter of fact. Our Rosen's been quite a womanizer. His wife was in a pretty bad way when Simon Bishop fell for her and pulled her out of it. And Rosen's got a guilt thing about that. He may be more scared about his daughter, that's only natural. But he's damn worried about his ex-wife, too."

Jarrell looked at her with grudging respect again. "He told you all that?"

"One of my assets as a reporter. People tell me things. Even quite personal things. Except you, of course. But I already know a lot about you; from the Congo, and things I heard afterwards. Gerd von Kleist may be the strangest of this crew; but you come a pretty close second. In a diametrically opposite way."

Jarrell's smile was amused. "The angel and the devil?"

"You flatter yourself, Jarrell. You're no devil. Just a man without moral convictions."

"You're quite sure of that, are you?"

"Uh-huh. You sell arms and yourself to any side that pays. In Katanga, they said you'd sell yourself to both sides at the same time, if you could."

Jarrell laughed softly. "That's true enough. So?"

Nora Devlin shrugged. "So that makes you a very cynical man. And cynicism's going out of style these days. That boy in there is neurotic, maybe even psychotic. But at least he makes a moral choice. He wages war for the side he believes is in the right."

"So did his father."

He waited for a sharp retort. There was none. He saw she was thinking about it. After a moment, she said: "That's true, of course. Interesting." She studied his night-shadowed face. "You're pretty bright. You ought to start thinking about using it for something with more meaning —and more of a future."

"Don't start mothering me, lady. It's not your style."

She went stiff, but he ignored it. His attention was suddenly turned in the direction of the shore, at a point where he'd seen something moving. Or thought he had. It was no longer there.

In two minutes Chalker would be late. Which wasn't like him.

Nora Devlin put aside her anger and looked off in the same direction. "Who's this man we're waiting for?"

"Floyd Chalker. And don't use *his* real name without permission. The United States army police would like to get their hands on him. He was a sergeant in the Green Berets. Career noncom. Got pretty badly wounded in Vietnam. After they patched him up, they put him to work running a G.I. bar. He sidelined into kick-backs and other assorted graft—and from that into selling perfectly good war materiel as used-up junk. Made a bundle—till the shit hit the fan, all over the front pages back in America."

Nora Devlin was nodding. "Which finally woke up Congress to what was going on. Damn good newspaper work, by reporters who knew how to dig. Landed some high brass and a lot of noncoms in jail."

"Chalker's one they didn't get. Skipped out in time, and made it to North Africa. Didn't manage to take much of his loot along, though. So he's been selling his services as a merc since then. And living in Morocco between times, quite decently. If a bit flashily. Has himself a sort of private little harem."

"If that's supposed to shock me, it doesn't. Your commando team gets more colorful by the minute."

Jarrell made an irritated sound. "Maybe that makes good copy for your newspapers, but you'll find colorful doesn't fit Floyd Chalker. He's just a very good soldier."

She read his accent on that quite accurately. "And that's the best thing a man can be, is that it?"

"Considering what we're going in there to do," he told her dryly, "you bet your sweet ass it is."

Guido called down softly from the flying bridge. "Something is coming—"

Jarrell scrambled up the outside ladder. He squinted in the direction Guido was pointing. After a moment he made it out: A boat, between them and the shore, coming their way. With its lights out, it was still too distant and shadowy to make out exactly what kind of boat.

"Signal him with two blinks," he told Guido. "And get ready to run for it if it's not him."

Dawn was splashing pink light across a slate-gray sky when the big Chevy station wagon carried them above the sea cliffs. It began following a narrow road that twisted and climbed through the Rif hills toward the house Chalker had been renting for the past two years outside the Berber village of Tarquist, forty miles southwest from Al Hoceima. Soon the arid coastal hills with their palm trees were left below, and they were into sweet-smelling forests of pines and cedars, watered by rushing mountain streams.

It was a deceptive foretaste of Morocco; nothing like the kind of country that lay beyond the Rif range to the south. Jarrell knew too well what waited for them down there.

He rode in front with Chalker. Rosen and Nora Devlin were in the seat behind them, Venturi and Gerd von Kleist in the one behind that. Floyd Chalker drove skillfully and listened without change of expression while Jarrell laid out the operation for him.

He was about thirty, and four inches taller than Jarrell; big in the bones and solidly padded with hard, serviceable muscle. His torso was unusually wide in the chest and shoulders, tapering down to a spare waist and narrow hips. He had a flat, stern slab of a face, hacked out of rough granite. His massive hands guided the wheel with surprising delicacy as he thought over the proposition.

"Five thousand bucks ain't a helluva lot," he stated finally, "for what you're talking about. Gonna be one fucking hard thing to—" He cut himself off and glanced back at Nora Devlin. "Excuse the language, ma'am. Forgot."

She laughed. "I don't shock that easy, soldier."

"Glad to hear it. But the apology stands." Chalker suddenly stopped the car, putting it in neutral but leaving the motor running. He turned his bulk around in the seat and fixed his gaze on Rosen. "I want more than five thousand bucks if I come in. I want Simon Bishop to use all them connections of his to get the U.S. government to drop the charges against me."

A surprisingly poignant note crept into his heavy voice. "I'm getting homesick. I want to be able to go back to Utah; at least for a visit."

"I'll pass the word," Rosen told him. "Bishop'll pull all the strings he has, that I guarantee. If anybody can swing something like that, he can."

Floyd Chalker continued to look Rosen in the eyes; with a searching stare that had scared platoons of troopers, and made officers carefully respectful.

Rosen didn't flinch worth a damn. He just stared back coldly. "I *said* I'll pass on the word."

Slowly, Chalker nodded, the granite face staying impassive. "Okay, Mr. Rosen. Good enough." He turned forward, put the station wagon in gear, and resumed driving. "It's a deal."

"Better arrange to get anything you want in your place shipped out," Jarrell told him. "If we do pull this one off, your chance of getting back in the country isn't too good."

"That, you don't have to tell me. All I got that I care about is some guns. We'll stop and pick 'em up at the house. And there's a guy waiting there I want you to meet. Name's Santiso Josal. I got in touch with him after Marcel phoned me from Nice. He's looking for a job."

Jarrell frowned a bit, thinking back. "Name doesn't ring a bell."

"I'm recommending him," Chalker said.

"That means he's good," Jarrell acknowledged. "But I want to know who he is. And what he is."

"Josal's from Guatemala. Got himself called the Butcher of Chiquimula, before he had to get out in a hurry." Chalker told Jarrell some more about Santiso Josal. It didn't make pleasant listening, for anybody with a queasy stomach.

There was an opening in a high stone wall on a wooded

slope. Beyond a graveled drive cut through a dense olive grove. It led to a white Spanish villa with a red-tiled roof, curved around a gold-and-black mosaic patio in which a swimming pool glittered in the morning light. It had been built, Chalker explained as he pulled into a small parking strip, by a businessman from Madrid who'd had to get out in a hurry along with the Spanish army when Abd-el-Krim's savage clans had swept through this area on their way to bloody glory at Tetouan. It had been renovated and the swimming pool put in by a Frenchman, before France had withdrawn its official and military presence from Morocco.

Chalker's contribution to the place was apparent when they left the station wagon and crossed the mosaic patio. Two nubile blondes were stretched out naked on multi-colored cushions beside the pool, finishing off their night's sleep and improving their overall suntans at the same time.

"Tourists from Sweden," Chalker commented offhandedly as he led them past. "Been here a while."

His voice didn't waken the girls. Nora Devlin glanced from their sprawled nudity to Floyd Chalker's stern face, having difficulty fitting them together. "I thought Jarrell was kidding me about your running a harem here."

Chalker's voice got stiffly formal: "I'm not a married man, Miss Devlin. No reason I shouldn't enjoy life, when I can."

The big ex-sergeant led them into a cool, marble-floored hall and pointed through a wide doorway. "Kitchen's that way. Why'nt the rest of you brew some coffee while I go wake Josal up."

Only Jarrell followed Chalker through to the rear of the house. He wasn't about to recruit Santiso Josal without sizing him up first.

They entered a large room dominated by a big, old-fashioned brass bed. No man was in sight. Just a small, dark girl curled up sound asleep in the middle of the mattress. She looked Malaysian. Jarrell noted a bruise on her sweetly curved buttocks, and tired circles under her eyes. "Looks like he gave her a hard night."

"Usually does. But she seems to like it, so—" Chalker

shrugged a massive shoulder and turned to have a look for Josal in the adjoining bathroom.

Gunshots exploded behind them. Jarrell spun toward the open French windows, poised to hit the floor. It had been a heavy-caliber rifle; two fast shots, blending together. But nothing was out there in the small back garden.

"No sweat," Chalker said soothingly. "Josal must be getting in some early target practice with my guns. To sharpen himself up for you."

"If he needs sharpening, I don't need him."

"See for yourself." Chalker headed out into the garden. Jarrell looked at the dark girl again before following. She was still dead to the world. The shots hadn't reached through her layers of exhausted sleep.

Beyond the garden there was a line of walnut trees, and beyond that the ground dipped into a short ravine. A line of small tin cans was set on a plank platform at one end of it. At the other end was a wooden table with a .38 service revolver and two open boxes of ammunition on it. Santiso Josal, wearing only a pair of dungarees, stood beside the table hefting an M16 automatic rifle with the change lever set for single-shot firing. He was a couple years younger than Chalker; almost as big and powerful.

He aimed and fired as Jarrell and Chalker came down into the ravine. A tin can jumped high off the plank platform at the other end. Josal fired again. The can spun to the left in midflight. Josal lowered the big rifle and grinned at Jarrell, showing small white teeth.

The brutality was concentrated around the mouth. The rest of his face was as smoothly innocent as a baby's. His eyes had about as much expression as two brown rivets.

According to Chalker, he had been called "the butcher" because of his success in one area of Guatemala as part of a secret police group known as the death squad—which specialized in hunting down and murdering rebel guerrillas. A political dispute turning out wrong had forced him to flee to Europe; with funds stolen from the secret police treasury. When the cash had run out, he'd begun selling his background training as a guerrilla hunter and killer in Africa; usually to the Portugese in Mozambique and Angola.

To Jarrell he looked about as evil a man as you could find even in Morocco. But that was one kind of man drawn to mercenary work. And in this operation Josal's kind of know-how could turn out useful.

Josal got tired of the way Jarrell was studying him. "You are not satisfied with my marksmanship?" he demanded in fairly good French. He smiled again to take the sting out, but there was hard arrogance in the voice.

"You're using a good rifle," was all Jarrell gave him. He'd noticed Rosen standing nearby, looking angry and troubled. Ignoring his presence for the moment, Jarrell asked Chalker: "What else've you got here?"

"An ugly little M3 submachine gun. Perfect for close-in work."

"The AR-18S is better. I'm hoping Lepic can locate one for me."

"If there're any around," Chalker said, "Mahjoub Lepic's the guy to find 'em. Bringing him in for the action, too?"

"If I can get him. He off on something else right now?"

"Not that I've heard."

Santiso Josal couldn't take being ignored. "If you don't want me, you will please say so. Now." He thumped the rifle down on the table. "I need a paying job, but I don't beg for it."

Jarrell saw that the arrogance had given way to stiff, easily hurt pride. "Let's see what you can do with the .38."

The empty brown eyes stayed on Jarrell's face for a second. Then Josal picked up the .38, turning into a neatly balanced stance and aiming without bothering to brace his gun hand with his other hand. He snapped off three quick shots.

Three of the tin cans at the other end of the ravine clanged off the platform. Josal didn't try to hit any of them again on the fly; and Jarrell hadn't expected him to, with a handgun. He never expected from another man what he couldn't do himself. Except with Gerd von Kleist.

Josal lowered the revolver and gave Jarrell a quizzical look. Before Jarrell could comment, Rosen was speaking, his voice almost shaking with impatience: "Dammit, Jarrell, what're you wasting all this *time* here for? We've got maybe ten days, at the most, to find Diana and Michele. Every minute we're not hunting them cuts their chances!"

Jarrell just looked at him for a moment. Then he said softly: "I told you at the start I understand your personal worry, but I won't let it influence my judgment of what to do and when to do it. I also told you if you came along, you'd have to follow orders. I'm giving you one now: Stand there and keep your mouth shut."

Jarrell waited and watched. It was rough, but he'd made up his mind he wasn't going any further if he had to argue each step of the way. He watched Rosen's fists clench, and then force themselves open. Rosen's mouth closed as he swallowed the words rising in his throat. Finally, he just nodded.

Jarrell relaxed. "While we're at it, can you do what Josal just did?"

Rosen looked at the two remaining tin cans at the other end of the ravine. "No," he said quietly, "not with the .38 at that distance. I'm not that good with a handgun."

Jarrell respected that. A good fighter knows exactly his own weaknesses and strengths. "And with a rifle?"

Rosen lifted the M16 off the table.

"Josal hit it on the fly," Jarrell told him pointedly.

Rosen didn't look at him. He tucked the butt of the stock to his shoulder, aimed, and fired. A tin can was smashed off the platform at the other end, hit a rock behind it and bounced. The rifle blasted again. The smashed can tore apart.

Jarrell took the rifle from Rosen. "You'll do." He looked to Santiso Josal. "Face me."

Josal turned his back on the ravine firing range.

"Catch and fire," Jarrell told him.

Josal just watched him, waiting.

Jarrell tossed the M16. Josal caught it two-handed, spun around, and fired before finishing the spin. The last tin can jumped crazily in the air. Josal's second bullet caught it before it was twelve inches off the plank.

Jarrell nodded slightly.

His army now numbered seven.

One more to go. Down in Marrakesh. Near the big square known as "the Meeting Place of the Dead."

SIX

The station wagon carried them up out of a stony, infertile land onto the Haouz plateau, flanked by the dead, yellowish remnants of Djebillet's volcanic hills. And there, suddenly ahead of them, lay one of the blood-stirring sights of Africa: Marrakesh, surrounded by a vast, lush-green palm oasis and eight miles of ocher-red fortress walls, topped by the towering Koutoubia minaret. With the gaunt, lofty splendor of the Atlas range for a backdrop.

The mountains rose, forty miles to the south and east, in sharp, harsh ridges clawing one above another into the sky; dropping down unseen on the other side into the limitless, eerie stretches of the Sahara Desert. Down through the centuries strange armies had come undetected out of that desert and through those mountains; to fall upon Marrakesh with the unexpectedness of a thunderclap on a clear day. In that same stretch of centuries succeeding governments had learned the impossibility of controlling the elusive tribes whose gatherings forever threatened; because of that same Atlas barrier, whose few narrow passes seemed designed for ambushes.

In another month the Atlas peaks would gleam with snow, though the sands on the other side were still burning. Now they were naked rock, hazy in the heat-shimmering air. Below the peaks the gaunt slopes looked empty of life; but their tortured folds contained mysteries not to be grasped from the relative safety of Marrakesh.

Including the forces gathering around Bel Zaara; and the fate of two American women in their hidden stronghold.

Jarrell continued to gaze reflectively at the mountains as he told Chalker which of the ten gates to take through the wall of the old city: the Bab Doukkala.

There was a jangle of chains and clashing of locks being drawn on the other side of the iron door to the windowless, unlighted cell. Michele Bishop and her daughter rose from the mattresses that had been placed on the damp stone floor for them. They groped for each other in the pitch darkness, clutched each other's hands.

It was less than an hour since they'd been fed, so the reason for their cell door being opened now was unknown to them. And the unknown was even more frightening than the terrors they already knew. They had no idea where they were. Only that it was somewhere deep under ground. They'd been brought most of the way blindfolded. What was above and around them was another unknown.

The heavy cell door screeched open on rusted, unoiled hinges. Michele and Diana were blinded by the glare of a kerosene lantern entering their cell. It was several seconds before they could make out the man carrying it: a stocky, darkly handsome man in the uniform of an army officer.

Colonel Omrani studied the hostages with a faint smile, enjoying the way they clung to each other and squinted fearfully into the light. It roused a latent sexual sadism in him.

He had been one of the officers caught on the wrong side of the last attempt to unseat the government; the most senior of the small group lucky enough to escape. He was grateful for that luck, and eager about the possibilities for himself in the new secret alliance. But he was also very bored so far from the pleasures he was accustomed to in the city. And here were two attractive, helpless women, whose possibilities were not being used.

He put the lantern on the floor and shook his head

sadly as he looked around. The cell was small, and everything was solid stone—walls, floor, ceiling. "This is really deplorable. Not a place for ladies like yourselves. Definitely not. I regret that very much. Perhaps," he added tentatively, "I *might* be able to have you moved to more suitable quarters. With windows, at least."

He knew that was quite impossible. When the government released the hundred prisoners, Bel Zaara would let these women go. They could not be allowed to return to civilization able to tell anything that could lead the army to this place.

Michele Bishop seemed to be reading his thoughts. She eyed him with hard suspicion. "What do you want here?"

His expression became hurt. "I? I want nothing but to help you. Try to make you and your daughter more comfortable."

Diana began to show a little hope. "Could you at least swing some sheets and blankets for—"

Her mother cut in, still watching Omrani suspiciously. "And what do you want in exchange for being that nice to us?"

Colonel Omrani just smiled.

"That's what I thought," Michele Bishop snapped. "Get the hell out of here!"

The colonel continued to smile. She had fire, this older one, in addition to beauty. He liked that. But he liked the daughter better. Not as lovely, but with the youth he craved more than other things in a female.

He cupped Diana's chin in his blunt hand and tilted her face to him. "About the sheets and blankets——"

Diana's right hand became a fist and struck his arm away. Hard enough to hurt. For a moment he just gaped at her. Then he slapped her across the face, sending her sprawling on one of the mattresses. Michele Bishop sprang at him, fingers clawing. He threw her against the wall, and began advancing on her. Then he froze.

Another man was in the cell. His coming had been so silent he seemed to have materialized out of the shadows. The hooded *djellabah* that flowed around his grossly fat form was pure white silk. His eyes were dark pits peering

70

through folds of pale flesh in a face ravaged by disease. Bel Zaara's uncle: Allal Ben Hafidi, ruler of one nomadic clan and leader of a growing number of others waiting on his word to rise throughout the Atlas and Sahara.

The disease seemed to have affected his vocal cords, too. His voice was a croak: "What do you do here, Omrani?"

It was asked mildly enough; but something in it made Colonel Omrani glance nervously at the huge black slave towering behind Ben Hafidi. Slavery was officially done away with in Morocco, of course; but the slave didn't know that. The Arab flesh-brokers had brought him from far to the south when very young, and he was not aware any other life was possible. He did know that his existence depended on serving well and instantly; so he kept his hand on the jeweled hilt of his lean, curved sword while he listened carefully to the tone of his master's voice and watched Omrani.

"I merely came down here," Colonel Omrani said blandly, "to see if these females were all right."

"And why should they not be?"

They were speaking in a language neither hostage could understand. But what was happening was obvious. Diana, sitting up on the mattress and holding her hurt cheek, suddenly burst out in her rudimentary French: "The son of a bitch came down here to——"

She was stopped by Michele whispering fiercely: "Be *quiet*, Diana——" Very aware that they didn't know the relationship between these men; nor which their fate might depend upon.

In the past, Diana would have ignored the command and gone on saying what she wanted to say. But she looked at Michele's face, and held back. There had been a sporadic undercurrent of hostility between them since Michele had married Bishop, destroying the vain hope that she might remarry Diana's father. But that was forgotten now, in their mutual danger.

The almost invisible eyes were fixed on Colonel Omrani from the depths of the dark pits. "You know what kind of death awaits these women if the government does not obey our demands within the time given," Allal Ben Hafidi

71

croaked. "But until then, my nephew has sworn they will not be harmed. In any way. The honor of my name stands behind the word of my nephew. It will not be broken. By anyone."

Omrani tried to keep his voice bland, but there was a tremor in it now: "I have no intention of breaking that word, I assure you, Ben Hafidi."

"Good. Then we have no further business here." Allal Ben Hafidi turned and waddled out, followed closely by the slave with the sword.

Colonel Omrani snatched up the lantern and hurried after them without a backward glance. The cell door clanged shut.

Solid darkness enclosed the hostages.

The Djemaa El Fna has been called "the Place of Marvels" and "the Pulsing Heart of Africa." But the name that sticks is "the Meeting Place of the Dead." A reminder of a time not long past when the *khalifa* of Marrakesh had shown the folly of rebellion against the Sultan by displaying the severed heads of captured rebels around the big square. Hordes of vultures had flown down and picked the heads clean of flesh. Each day fresh heads had been added to the grisly display. By the time the rebellion died out, there were literally hundreds of naked skulls staring at each other across the vast Djemaa El Fna.

The skulls were no longer there, but the memory lingered. A memory sharpened for Jarrell by what they'd found happening around them since arriving. Marrakesh was steaming with intrigue and fear. Police, troops, and secret security men were combing the city day and night in an intensified search for rebel elements, snatching up suspects and dragging them off to interrogation cells.

Each member of Jarrell's group had been stopped several times on the day they'd arrived. But since their false papers showed them to be harmless tourists, and the police knew them now, they were no longer bothered.

The large number of cops wandering in and out of the Djemaa El Fna was not the only thing new about this vast open area in the old medina inside the walls. Though half of it remained a market filled with shops, cafés, and little tent-shaded stalls, the other half had been turned into a parking area and taxi stand. And some of the performers who'd traditionally entertained the thousands swarming in the square were now banned; fortune tellers, and the little boys doing erotic dances.

But otherwise nothing basic had changed; not in eight hundred years. Marrakesh was still the terminal for caravans from as far south as the Niger and as far east as the Indian Ocean. And the Djemaa El Fna was still its colorful heart; recalling for Jarrell with shocking sharpness the colors of forgotten memories:

The burning yellow of a sea of sand, separated only by a thin circle of distant horizon from a sky the same color.

The sick loathing of the color green, which had lasted for almost a year after dragging what was left of his ambushed unit through a fetid tropical swamp.

A whitewashed room, with a girl shrouded in black except for her frightened eyes and gold harlot-slippers.

He sat with Rosen, Gerd and Venturi at a small hotel terrace on the edge of the square, taking it all in: The mind-boggling conglomeration of camels, trucks, donkeys, taxis, goats, sheep, cars, mules, buses, horses. The haze of reddish dust stirred up by the thousands shuffling out of the confusing cobwebbing of crooked streets and alleys in the surrounding medina—pale Moors from the farm villages and dusky mountain Berbers; black Sudanese and Sengalese up from the jungles, and blue-tinted Taureg camel drivers out of the deserts. The crowds formed islands around acrobats, fire-eaters, and chanting holy beggars, shifting to create pathways for water-carriers with their tinkling brass cups and strolling musicians with their weird five-tone music accompanied by pounding Sudanese drums.

And a sprinkling of Europeans; utterly alien beings almost lost in this noisy, congested human whirlpool.

Jarrell sipped a traditional mint tea and glanced off to the right of the terrace, to the outdoor café where Nora Devlin was nursing her third glass of Thessala wine. She was searching the native faces swirling past her, looking for the face of the man who'd been Bel Zaara's contact to her the last time. And she was alone; because if the contact did show up, he might be frightened off if he saw unknown men with her.

It was almost evening, and she'd been at it since early morning. With no more luck than she'd had late the day before, after they'd arrived. Almost two days, and she was still watching and waiting. While the time left to them ran out, and her news story with it.

And the lives of Michele Bishop and Diana Rosen.

Slouched beside Jarrell, Marcel Venturi was brooding on the same dark thought while he nibbled a date from the bowl on their table. On the other side of Jarrell, Rosen sat with his cup of syrupy *kawa* untasted. With the relentless leaking away of time and hope, Rosen was beyond angry anxiety. He just stared ahead of him, watching some horror the others couldn't see. Except, perhaps, for Gerd von Kleist, who watched Rosen with a peculiar intensity; as though trying somehow to absorb the pain into himself, and thus free the older man of it.

Santiso Josal was off prowling a section of the Kasbah where he had friends, inside the Bab Ksiba; Floyd Chalker was checking out contacts in the new city outside the walls. Both trying to track down some kind of lead to Bel Zaara.

Mahjoub Lepic, who'd agreed to come in, was also digging for a lead; and he was the one most likely to come up with something. But so far even Lepic had had as little luck with his digging as Nora Devlin with her vigil. Marrakesh was a scared city; anybody with the slightest connection to suspected subversives was already in a secret police cell, if they hadn't gotten out of town or found a hole to hide in.

"There's no point in staying here any more," Venturi said in a soft, flat voice. "This contact the Devlin girl knows isn't going to show up. I wouldn't, if I were him. Not with all these cops around."

Jarrell shot a look at Rosen. But Rosen seemed not to have heard. He went on staring straight ahead, into his private hell.

"We've got four chances of turning something up this way," Jarrell told Venturi. "Lepic, Chalker, Josal—and the girl there."

"But it isn't working," Venturi pointed out quietly. "So maybe we should change tactics? You're the boss, Earl. I'm only suggesting—We could go up in the mountains with Lepic, to that tribe his mother belonged to. Maybe get a lead that way."

Jarrell had thought about it. He glanced at his watch and stood up. "Lepic's supposed to be waiting for me about now. He could have something."

"And if he does not?"

"Then I'll *have* to find another way. In the meantime, keep an eye on her." Jarrell glanced toward Nora Devlin, got a blank look in return, and turned away through the crowded square.

Working his way past a group clustered around an open tent in which a dentist was pulling teeth from a groaning patient, he entered a twisting alley and left the Djemaa El Fna behind. Soon he was deep within the medina; two square miles of ancient native quarters jumbled together. The lowering sun turned it into a complicated puzzle of red-brown houses and black streets, none of which went in the same direction for more than twenty feet.

If he hadn't known the route so well, Jarrell would have been utterly lost within seconds. He threaded through a labyrinth of convoluted passageways and interlocking, blind-walled buildings concealing hidden courtyards and gardens. Here, everything was like that: impenetrably secretive, slightly sinister. And thick with the smells of a medieval Orient, blending violently in air trapped between close-packed walls. The smells of figs and almonds, of dung and urine, of bitter brewing coffee and too-sweet dough boiling in rancid oils. And occasional whiffs of hashish and incense from latticed windows.

Jarrell reached the small square of the dyers' *souk*. He took his time strolling around it, admiring the brilliant colors of the huge skeins of wool hanging out to dry on ropes strung between roof tops. Red, yellow, and blue dye dripped from them, making livid splashes on the uneven cobbles. A complete circuit didn't reveal any over-zealous secret police type following him out of curiosity. But he checked again when he got to the metal-workers' *souk,* buying a brass candlestick while he looked in a tin-framed mirror hung up for sale. No one was tailing him.

Swinging the candlestick carelessly in one hand, Jarrell turned into a particularly sordid alley reeking of donkeys and cats. It was floored with dirt, and burrowed between cracking walls without a single window or doorway.

The walls tilted crazily as they reared higher. Their jutting roofs almost blocked out all light. Heavy arches, just above Jarrell's head, kept the walls from falling and made the passageway even darker. Jarrell turned a sharp corner into another alleyway. A beggar in a tattered black burnoose huddled in the dirt against the wall, sounding a mournful wail on an oboelike instrument called a *rhaita.* He held it to his toothless mouth with hands that had no fingers.

It was a stupid place for a beggar to be, and there were no coins in the wicker bowl on his folded legs. Jarrell put the candlestick in it and went past. Behind him the *rhaita* continued its monotonous wail. If the beggar had never seen Jarrell before the tone of the wailing would have changed subtly; and someone within hearing would have hurried through some secret hole to warn Mahjoub Lepic.

There was a heavy, rusted iron door set in a thick wall of crumbling bricks covered with old vines. The door looked as if it hadn't been used in decades. A scrawny old man wrapped in a cloak and hood that were a collection of rags sat on the ground beside this door. He was smoking *kif* in a reed pipe, his eyes dazed and bloodshot.

Jarrell nudged him out of his drugged dreams with the toe of his boot. "Open up, Mulay."

"Na'am Sidi." The old man's voice was slurred and his eyes stayed unfocused. But he struggled near enough to the surface to drag himself to his feet and get a large wrought-iron key from inside his rags. He unlocked the rusted iron door, which swung open smoothly, without

a squeak. Jarrell stepped inside and shut it behind him; heard it being relocked.

There was another wall in front of him. A narrow passage led to left and right between the two walls. This was a neighborhood where many buildings had fallen into disuse, while others had been incorporated into houses around them. The way left led to a maze of ruins. Jarrell went to the right, his shoulders brushing the walls on either side of him.

It led into a small, uncared-for courtyard, overgrown with high weeds that had broken through once lovely mosaics of the flooring. In the middle was a fountain that no longer flowed, its cracked stone bowl filled with brown moss and dead leaves from a single drooping palm.

Tiles cracked under Jarrell's weight as he crossed the abandoned court. Behind a bush on the other side, there was a hole where part of an ancient wall had collapsed. Jarrell had to bend to get through. On the other side was a dreary, empty room, its floor thick with dust where it had not collapsed into the dirt below. Lizards scuttled across plaster walls dissolving back to dust. The once colorful traceries that could still be made out near the ceiling were faded and covered with cobwebs. The windows and single doorway were boarded over from the outside.

A sliver of wood lay against a wall. Jarrell picked it up, and slid it through a slit in the door boardings. A metal bar lifted on the other side. Jarrell pushed the boarding open, and stepped into a short dark corridor. He walked to the end of it, turned a corner.

Beyond was the splendor of a blue-and-yellow tiled courtyard with marble columns and painted plaster embroidery on snowy white walls, surrounding an ornate stone and bronze fountain from which bubbling water splashed under the shade of two fruit-bearing lemon trees. From this, a graveled path bordered by cypress trees and vine-covered trellises led Jarrell to a larger and more splendid courtyard. This one was the heart of an old palace that had been renovated and well cared for. It was overhung by a second-floor gallery with ornate wooden columns and intricately carved arches.

77

Mahjoub Lepic was up there between two columns supporting a painted arch, waiting for him. He was tall and wire-thin; gorgeously attired in a flowing black silk *djellabah* trimmed with silver thread, over which he wore an open *selham,* a red velvet cloak embroidered with gold lace. His hood was flung back to reveal a round solid head with short-cropped red hair, and a dark, sardonic face with cool-humored gray eyes and a lean fierce mouth.

His father had been a sergeant in the Foreign Legion; his mother a mountain Berber. It was not the kind of match approved of by either the French general staff or the Berber elders. But Berber women were notoriously independent where sex was concerned, frequently bedding quite a number of men before taking the one they chose. Mahjoub Lepic's father had deserted from the Legion, spending the rest of his life in the Atlas with the tribe of his wife.

Berber women were called Daughters of the Night; which made Lepic one of the Sons of the Shadows. It fitted. The soft rich clothing he wore now, and the jeweled rings adorning the lean hand that beckoned Jarrell up, were deceptive. He was a creature of stealth and violence. Fencing stolen goods and smuggling were his joint trades; combining in his speciality of getting looted archeological treasures out of the country for sale in Europe. At times the brigand gangs he met on his way wanted everything, instead of their usual percentage fee for allowing passage through their territories. That Mahjoub Lepic had always won through was one factor recommending him to Jarrell. Another was his unusual knowledge of the secret ways through the mountains and across the borders. Still another was that the tribe of Lepic's mother was traditional blood enemy to the clan ruled by Bel Zaara's uncle, Allal Ben Hafidi.

Lepic motioned to an open doorway as Jarrell reached the top of a yellow-tiled stairway. "I could only find one AR submachine gun. But I got everything else on your list."

They stepped into a small room. Jarrell looked at the

weapons and ammo in open boxes, and at the other items he'd ordered. His eyes had a hard, sullen sheen as they returned to Mahjoub Lepic's dark face.

Lepic made an angry hissing sound through his teeth. "I know. None of this is any use unless we find where they are hidden."

"Which you haven't."

Lepic shook his head. "I regret, no. This is a bad time. There are not many left whom even I can question directly in such a matter. But I will try again this night. And perhaps—"

He didn't finish, and he didn't sound hopeful.

At that moment, all around them, muffled by the building walls, sounded the call of *muezzins* from the city's minarets, metallically resonant through P.A. amplifiers, echoing through the streets and over the buildings from one mosque to another: *"La illaha Allah wa-Muhammad rasul ullah . . . !"*

Summoning the faithful to evening prayers.

Jarrell looked through a small window that faced south, across the domes and towers and flat red roofs of Marrakesh. In the distance, beyond the old ramparts, the base of the Atlas range was already invisible in the spreading dusk. But the peaks flamed with gold. They would continue to do so long after Marrakesh was shrouded in night.

He kept his eyes on them as he spoke, his voice flat and harsh. "We're running out of time. We're going to have to go in there and find them. The hard way."

The skinny little Arab emerged nervously from his hiding place among the flowered bushes in the Mamounia gardens. He made his way through the deepening shadows of evening toward the Djemaa El Fna. His name was Ali ben Rehamna, and the hood of his rough brown wool burnoose was drawn close to partially conceal a face deeply pitted by smallpox scars. But he couldn't conceal the limp of a leg never properly set after it was broken in a fall from a camel when he was a child.

The crowd in the Djemaa El Fna had thinned considerably, as the devout went off to their evening prayers. That left those who were not so devout. But as Ali had expected, the armed police were all gone, to study the faces entering and leaving the mosques. Nevertheless, Ali remained nervously wary as he limped across the square, in the direction of a closed barber shop. A message was to be left there for a secret agent from Syria. He was half-way across when he saw the European woman coming toward him.

Her movements in his direction were uncertain. But he made the mistake of pausing and staring at her, startled as he recognized the reporter he'd led to Bel Zaara. That gave her too good a look at his face. Her approach became certain, and swift.

Ali shifted direction and angled away from her, toward the parking area. But he'd paused too long, and she was very quick. Her hand caught his arm, stopping him. "Wait," she whispered fiercely. "You remember me. You took me to Bel Zaara."

Ali looked around them in an agony of fear. "I do remember. But there are too many eyes here." He seized on the first thing that came to him: "Let me go and I will meet you later, in another place."

She continued to hold him, her face stubborn. "Bel Zaara *wanted* you to take me to him last time. He'll want it again. I come from someone who wants to give a great deal of money to Bel Zaara's cause. If you don't help me, he'll be very angry with you."

That got to Ali. He hesitated, then whispered: "Do you know the Al-Hamra Hotel? I will meet you there."

This time she believed him. "I'll find it."

"In the alley behind it. At midnight." Ali pulled his arm from her grasp and hurried away from her. He continued to the parking area, not wanting to approach the barber shop while she was watching.

He was in among the parked cars when a heavy-set man in a plain gray European suit appeared in front of him, blocking the way. Ali didn't know him, but he knew the look: a secret security detective.

Turning to run, Ali saw a uniformed policeman emerge

from the shadows among the cars behind him, drawing a revolver. Ali dodged off to the left. A man in a black suit stepped from behind a parked bus and swung a black-jack against the side of his head. Ali fell to the ground, moaning as he struggled to rise. The blackjack descended again. He sprawled on his face, twitched, and then lay still.

Nora Devlin stood rooted in the middle of the Djemaa El Fna, staring. The man in the gray suit was coming toward her, but she didn't run. She did what any normal tourist would do under the circumstances: stayed there and watched in surprise the way the policeman and the man in the black suit were dragging her contact's un-conscious figure to an unmarked Ford sedan.

The man in the gray suit came to a halt facing Nora, his hand held palm up. "Your papers, please."

She fumbled in the pocketbook that hung by a strap from her shoulder. "What's happening? What's that all about?"

Not answering, the security man studied her false passport, looking from her photo to her face. "What were you talking to Ali ben Rehamna about?"

"Who?"

His lips twitched with annoyance. "I am an officer of the state security branch. Do not play the fool. I am speaking of the man you were just talking to."

"I didn't know his name." That much was true enough. "I thought he might be able to tell me about some in-teresting places to see here at night."

The security man gazed at her with complete disbelief. "You thought he was a guide?"

"No, I just thought he was a native who'd know places most tourists don't see."

"And what did he tell you?"

Nora forced an embarrassed laugh. "That there were plenty of tourist offices around that would tell me about Marrakesh night life. But of course what I'm interested in is the sort of place the tourist offices *don't* tell you about. He said he didn't know the city well enough to help me, and walked off. And that's it. Now, what *is* this all about?"

The security man dropped her passport inside his jacket pocket. "You will come with me, please."

She looked puzzled. "I don't understand. What for? Where?"

"You will come with me," he repeated, politely but firmly.

There was no choice. As she accompanied him toward the Ford sedan, she shot a glance toward the hotel terrace. There, just before spotting Ali, she'd seen Santiso Josal join Rosen, Venturi, and Gerd.

Their table was empty.

SEVEN

Gerd von Kleist stepped out of an alleyway and stopped Jarrell as he approached the Djemaa El Fna in the gathering dusk. Quickly, he told him what had just happened. "Rosen said to get back to Mahjoub Lepic's house and wait there. He said you must not worry, he is taking appropriate action, with Venturi and Josal."

"*Rosen* said that?"

Gerd nodded, a bit puzzled. "I will tell you something odd, Jarrell. I believed him."

"They say *what* appropriate action?"

"No. Venturi just said this is one sort of thing the three of them know more about handling than I do."

"That's true enough," Jarrell said tightly. "Get back to Lepic and tell him. I'll bring in Chalker."

It was the only thing left for him to do, under the circumstances. He angled away from the Djemaa El Fna, heading for the Bab Djedid and the casino outside the walls, where Chalker should be by this time. Everything now depended on a worried little American with his anti-Gestapo experience some thirty years behind him, a mobster who might or might not be getting too old and slow for this kind of trick, and a sadistic former government cop who was more used to being on the other side in tangles of this sort.

The unmarked government car slowly negotiated a tight

turn in a narrow street at the edge of the medina, angling to take Avenue Mohammed V out through the walls to Internal Security headquarters in the new city. The uniformed cop was driving, with a still dazed Ali between him and the security agent in the black suit. The man in gray was in the back seat with Nora Devlin. Around the other side of the turn, they found the way blocked by a burro sagging under two immense burlap sacks of almonds.

The police driver pounded the horn and leaned out his side window, yelling for the farmer with the burro to get it out of there.

Rosen stepped out of a dark doorway and clubbed the driver unconscious with a short length of iron pipe.

Santiso Josal appeared at the other open front window, poking a black Luger through and touching the muzzle against the ear of the man in the black suit.

The security man in back with Nora made a grab for the inside of his opened jacket. He froze when he saw Marcel Venturi's cold eyes looking at him down the barrel of a Colt .45 automatic.

"Get out," Venturi told him silkily.

"You, too," Josal snapped at the security agent in front.

The one in back was out first. Rosen's pipe swung again, and he dropped against the rear tire, sprawling away from it unconscious. Nora Devlin scrambled from the car.

The security agent in black had his front door partly open by then. He kicked it the rest of the way open, making Josal jump back as he came out of the front seat yanking a pistol from a belt holster. The noise of the Luger was very loud in the confines of the narrow, walled-in street. The security man fell against the side of the car with his shoulder smashed, his pistol bouncing on the ground between his feet.

Josal cursed him and kicked him, very hard, in the stomach. The security man spilled to the ground doubled up in agony, clutching at his middle with his good hand as he rolled on his side. He stopped doing anything at all after the heel of Josal's boot cracked savagely across the side of his skull.

Rosen was already pulling the dazed Ali out of the front seat and was holding him up. Ali's legs were rubbery, and he still hadn't quite taken in what was happening. Josal ran around the front of the car to help. Between them, Rosen and Josal rushed Ali off down an alley.

Venturi waved his big .45 around in warning, and the few people stupid enough to still be out in sight vanished. Then he turned and ran for it with Nora. They were some distance away before she remembered that her passport was still in the security cop's pocket.

By then a police whistle had begun shrilling an alarm somewhere behind them.

In the night, a lantern burned at the top of each minaret, like a sprinkling of yellow stars hanging low over the darkness of the old city spread beneath. The Djemaa El Fna was silent and deserted now; the shops closed, the stalls and entertainers gone, not even a stroller to be seen. Even the crooked tangles of streets inside the medina were empty—except for armed police and army units, combing through them in an intensive house-by-house search. The usual night prowlers of the medina were keeping out of their way, moving through hidden passages to avoid the spread of the manhunt.

The picture of Nora Devlin on her false passport, Lepic's spies reported, had been reproduced and spread around—along with descriptions of Ali, Rosen, Venturi, and Josal. They were enemies of the state; and Marrakesh had become a massive trap for all of them.

Deep within that trap, little light escaped from the shuttered windows of Mahjoub Lepic's house. Behind one of those shutters, Jarrell, Rosen, and Nora sat in a smallish room around Ali, who was reclining on heavy cushions looking ill from the pain in his head. Jarrell watched Ali's face carefully as Nora repeated the reason he must take them to Bel Zaara. Rosen sat grim and quiet, merely nodding when she explained that he was the man prepared to contribute a large sum to the rebel cause. He looked tired from the letdown after what he'd done; but straining to get on with the objective it had made possible.

"*Why*," Ali demanded of Rosen, "should a foreigner like you wish to help our cause?"

"That," Rosen said flatly, "is for Bel Zaara's ears only."

In spite of his ingrained suspicion, Ali was inclined to believe them. First of all, because Bel Zaara had been extremely pleased by Nora Devlin's previous meeting with him. Second because these people had saved him from the police, at great risk to themselves; even shooting one of them. So they were obviously no friends to the government.

"But why are there so many of you? All men who look to me to be fighting men."

"We *are* fighting men," Jarrell told him. "Do you think the government wants your cause aided? They'll do anything they can to stop Mr. Rosen from reaching Bel Zaara. We're prepared to fight our way through, if we have to."

That, too, made sense to Ali. And he no longer had any intention of trying to deliver the message to the agent in the Djemaa El Fna. Marrakesh had become much too dangerous for him to stick around. "But unfortunately, I do not know where Bel Zaara is. Not exactly."

There was a short silence as they looked at him.

"You took me to him last time," Nora pointed out.

"No. *I* took you only as far as a certain village in the mountains. Another man lives there who does know where Bel Zaara is. *He* took you the rest of the way. I waited until he returned you to the village."

Mahjoub Lepic came into the room at that moment, his rich attire discarded for a common hooded burnoose of coarse cloth and desert boots. He was carrying a steaming cup, which he gave to Ali. "Drink this. It will take away the pain and give you sleep."

Jarrell shot him a searching glance. "Is there time for him to sleep?"

"So far the search has not entered this quarter. If it

does, we'll be warned." Lepic saw that Ali was looking at the cup without drinking, and snarled: "It is only mint tea with a little opium in it. If we were going to poison you, would we have rescued you?"

Ali sipped nervously at the tea while Jarrell filled Lepic in on what had been said. Lepic questioned Ali closely, then nodded.

"I know this village of the man he says is in contact with the guerrillas around Bel Zaara."

"How long'll it take to get there?" Rosen asked grimly.

"At least a day. It is very high, in terrain that makes the approach difficult."

"We can't risk trying to get out of this city in daylight," Jarrell said. "We have to do it tonight, or we lose another day we can't afford."

Lepic nodded. "A few hours before dawn will be safest. I'll arrange for transport."

Ali finished his drugged tea and leaned his head back carefully against the cushions. Jarrell rose to his feet. "Then there's time for all of us to get a little sleep. Our last one in comfort, for a while."

As they left the room, Jarrell noted a heavy-set Moor lounging in a chair against the corridor wall, with a curved dagger in his belt scabbard. Insurance that Ali would stay put, if the opium didn't do it.

The others were still in the large *divan,* where they'd all dined on the excellent couscous Lepic's cook had served up. They lowered their drinks and stared at Nora. She was hardly recognizable, in a homespun *djellabah.* With the hood partially shadowing her face and concealing her hair, she could pass for a teenage Berber or Arab boy.

"My disguise," she explained with mock solemnity as she sat down to join them. "Too many Marrakesh cops have my picture by now."

"And," Lepic added, "she will be less conspicuous in the mountains this way."

Gerd von Kleist froze in the act of pouring a glass of wine for Nora. He stared at Jarrell. "You're taking her in *there* with us?"

87

It was Nora who answered first. "I'm covering this story, start to finish. If any of you are thinking of leaving me behind at this stage, forget it."

"Besides," Rosen pointed out as he lowered himself to some cushions and pulled over a whiskey bottle, "she's still our best passport to Bel Zaara, if he's willing to make a deal."

"Anyway," Jarrell said, "she wouldn't be safe here. So she *has* to go with us, and get out with us."

"You make it sound like you're doing her a favor," Gerd said angrily. "You know Lepic could get her smuggled out of the country, some easy way."

Jarrell looked at him without expression. "She goes with us. That's final. No further discussion, Gerd." Jarrell took the bottle out of Rosen's hand, drank from it, and forced everything out of his mind except an assessment of the obstacles ahead; and the tactics for overcoming them.

But Floyd Chalker was looking troubled, too. "Where we're going," he told Nora, "really can be a rough thing for a woman. I found a girl in there once. After some of the bandits that watch the passes had gotten finished with her. She was dead by then, thank God. The things they'd done to her, with knives and—" Chalker stared soberly into his glass, not finishing it.

Santiso Josal nodded. "Berbers can be pretty sadistic." He remembered and looked quickly at Lepic. "No offense, Mahjoub."

"No offense taken. It's true, but not that simple. There's as much masochism as sadism in it. It's something pagan from our past; from even before the Arabs invaded our land. There are still some who get a strange religious-sexual ecstasy, out of *getting* pain as much as in giving it."

Rosen grimaced with distaste. "Including you?"

Mahjoub Lepic shuddered faintly. "No."

Gerd was looking at him with interest. "All religion has some trace of it, you know," he said softly. "A penance for the sins of the past. It has to be understood in its context."

Marcel Venturi made a sound of angry impatience. "Of course *you* understand. Germans are specialists in that kind of insanity. That 'penance' of yours is going to get you killed one of these days. Or leave you a cripple the rest of your life, the kind of chances you take."

Gerd shrugged. "That is in God's hands."

Chalker studied him uncomfortably. "You really are crazy, like they say. You know that?"

"Perhaps."

"My father was much the same as Gerd, once," Lepic put in mildly. "He had even had a scorpion tattooed on his cheek, so he could never return to face whatever secret made him join the Foreign Legion."

Nora's interest sharpened. "How'd your mother feel about always having to look at a scorpion on his face?"

"She thought it was lovely. Her face was tattooed, too; strictly abstract art, of course. All Berber women have that done, while they are still little girls."

Nora shook her head disgustedly. "Lots of women, all over the world, still do things that are pretty much the same. Anything that will get men to notice them."

Lepic gave her a small smile. "Berber women don't wait around to be noticed. When it comes to sex, *they* are the aggressors. My mother took one look at my father, tried him out, and then made him desert the Legion and took him home with her."

"Did your father ever tell you what he had done, that he had to join the Legion?" Venturi asked curiously.

"No. The Legion says they all join for the same reason: to die. But my father once told me his idea had been 'to mortify the flesh, until the brain can't remember.'"

Gerd nodded slowly, understanding it well.

"But whatever it was," Lepic added, "he got over it."

"Then," Gerd said flatly, "it could not have been very deep."

"Deep enough. But some things go deeper." Lepic laughed. "You don't know Berber women."

Nora Devlin sighed. "You know what?" she stated with some humor. "The more time I spend with the bunch of you, the more I'm convinced you're all crazy."

"But of course, my dear," Josal told her with a slight bow. "We are a small band of disciplined madmen."

Jarrell stood up, stretching like a sleepy panther. "Don't talk rot, Josal, if you can help it. You're just soldiers on a mission."

Lepic looked at him. "But soldiers have always romanticized what they do, or they would not be able to do it. It helps, sometimes, to believe one is inspired by a kind of divine insanity, of the fallen on a brief visit from hell."

"That's very poetic," Jarrell told him dryly. "Now what about that transport you were going to arrange?"

Lepic looked smiling from him to Nora. "You understand, of course? It embarrasses him. *His* feelings run too deep for words." Rising to his feet, he strolled from the room.

Nora looked after him, and then thoughtfully at Jarrell. She didn't say anything.

The house of Mahjoub Lepic was intricately laid out, with enough rooms for Nora to have one all to herself to sleep in. She slept soundly, as she'd learned to sleep between actions when covering the Vietnam War for her news service. It was still deep night when a hand squeezed her shoulder and wakened her.

Opening her eyes, she saw Jarrell's shadowed face hovering over her in the darkness of the room.

"Get up," he told her softly. "Somebody spotted you coming in here. There're cops all around the place. They'll be breaking in any second."

EIGHT

Jarrell turned out of the room and strode quietly through the unlit corridor.

Nora hurried after him. "If they've surrounded the house, how do we get out?"

"That's Lepic's department." His voice was careless, almost indifferent. He moved differently now, she noted; with a kind of slouched, gathering power. It wasn't until they were out on the second-floor gallery overlooking the central courtyard that she became aware of the Walther P-38 automatic his right hand held down beside his leg.

The courtyard below was dark and empty. But something hard was pounding against reinforced wood, somewhere off to their right. Jarrell led her to the left, into another dark corridor that twisted deep inside Lepic's complex of interconnecting buildings. It made a sharp turn, and abruptly they were out on a small balcony with steps leading down into a short, brick-paved passage. Some starlight filtered through an opening in the roof.

There was an open door at each end of the passage. Lepic came hurrying out of one, heading for the other. He was followed by Chalker and Josal, lugging a heavily loaded open box between them. Gerd von Kleist came through behind them, looking back with an almost eager tension. He was carrying a pump-action repeating shotgun and his pockets bulged with extra shells. The thirteen-round Browning H-P automatic he favored was in an open kid holster clipped to his belt on his left hip.

Lepic paused as he saw Jarrell coming down the steps to them with Nora. "This is the last of it. The other boxes are through."

Jarrell stuck his Walther automatic inside his belt and snatched the stubby Armalite submachine gun from the box. "How long'll you need?"

"Two, three minutes." Lepic hurried on through the other doorway.

Jarrell got two of the curved twenty-round magazines from the box as Josal and Chalker carried it past him after Lepic. "Go with them," he told Nora, and looked to Gerd. "Take the corner behind you."

Gerd backed into the deeply shadowed corner, watching the door he'd come out of, as Jarrell went back up onto the balcony two steps at a time. Jarrell snapped one of the ammo magazines into the Armalite and dropped the other in a pocket of his loose-hanging bush jacket as he reentered the dark corridor. The submachine gun carried lightly, less than eight pounds, even with the fully loaded magazine attached. And with its shortened barrel and the stock folded in as it was now, it was less than thirty inches long. If he had to start delivering a lot of fire-power in these close quarters, he couldn't do better.

At the other end of the corridor, he stopped just inside the dark doorway. Holding himself utterly motionless, he looked past the gallery into the central courtyard. It was still empty. Jarrell hefted the submachine gun in both hands and listened. The house was silent now, except for water splashing in the fountain below. He waited, one part of his mind automatically attuned to the precise passage of seconds in the three minutes Lepic had asked for. His heart thudded heavily against his ribs; the old tightness was back in his throat, the old taste in his mouth.

Below and off to the left, there was the noise of a door splintering open. A muscle jerked in Jarrell's cheek. His hands grasped the submachine gun's pistol grips almost caressingly. Once he'd made tests with an AR–18S, before buying a shipment for resale in Aden. At two hundred and fifty yards it could drive its .223 bullets clear through one man and into another. At three hundred and sixty yards they would still punch through a steel helmet.

Two troopers came down the shadowy path toward the courtyard, advancing warily with their automatic rifles pointing the way. Jarrell watched them with narrowed eyes, the lean flesh over his cheekbones drawn very taut. They paused at the edge of the court, looking around quickly, unsure. There were so many dark doorways facing the courtyard, they didn't know where to head first. Raising their heads, they scanned the upper gallery. At one point each of them looked directly at the dark doorway containing Jarrell. But at that distance his utter stillness made him invisible.

An officer came along the path, followed by eight more soldiers with automatic weapons. He snapped quiet orders, gesturing with a revolver. Five of the troopers fanned across the courtyard to investigate the many lower doorways and the maze of rooms behind them. The officer led the other five up the stairway to the second-floor gallery.

Jarrell drew himself further inside the darkness of his doorway. Most of the seconds were gone by now. He turned and went swiftly through the corridor, his rubber-soled boots making no sound on the tiles.

Gerd was exactly as he'd left him, merged in the shadow of his corner below, the repeating shotgun held with seeming carelessness in his right hand, its barrel hanging down. Jarrell motioned to him from the little balcony. The shotgun barrel swung up and was cupped in Gerd's left hand, aimed at the end of the passage through which the troopers searching the ground-floor rooms would emerge, sooner or later. Otherwise he didn't move.

Jarrell backed as far as he could along the balcony, put his shoulders against the wall there, and centered his attention and the Armalite on the doorway to the upper corridor, listening for footsteps inside it.

More seconds leaked past. It was taking more than three minutes.

Mahjoub Lepic appeared at the end of the passage behind Gerd and hissed softly. Jarrell put a hand on the balcony railing and vaulted over, dropping to the brick paving below with his feet spread and the give of his knees absorbing the shock. Gerd backed past him into Lepic's doorway with the shotgun still held ready. Jarrell stepped in backward after them and shut the door. They were in total darkness, until Lepic snapped on a flashlight he was carrying. Jarrell followed its light down a flight of narrow stone steps.

At the bottom Lepic opened another door. A cloud of hot steam gushed out at them. Jarrell, the last to enter, closed the door again. The room was filled with steam, through which an invisible lamp cast a diffused yellow glow. They were in a *hamman,* the Moorish steam bath found in many wealthy Moroccan homes. Through the drifting steam, Jarrell made out the vague, huge-bellied shape of a naked man stretched out on a stone platform. He was filling a tin cup with water from a curved pipe rising out of the tiled floor, and pouring it on his face and head.

"One of my uncles," Lepic explained. "He'll signal on the pipe when they come this way. And get indignant enough to delay them a bit."

He was already opening a door on the other side of the *hamman.* They stepped through, shut and locked it. Lepic's flashlight guided them down another flight of stone steps.

They were into a deep cellar now. The huge round mouth of an old well was sunk in its stone floor, plunging into blackness. A rusty iron grille covering had been tilted away from it. Lepic flashed his light into the well, and Jarrell saw iron rungs sunk into the curved stones, leading down.

"Pull the grille back in place after us," Lepic said, and climbed down into the well.

As Gerd went in after him, Jarrell looked up and located the pipe running up through the ceiling to the spigot from which Lepic's uncle was getting his water. Hanging the submachine gun over his shoulder by its canvas sling, Jarrell started down the iron rungs. He paused with his boots planted on the third one, got hold of the grille with both hands, and dragged it into place over his head as he descended another rung.

There was a faint clanking sound from the ceiling above. Lepic's uncle was rapping the tin cup against his end of the pipe, in the *hamman*. Jarrell continued his descent into the depths of the well.

His legs were in bottom water up to the knees when he found that one of the big stones that formed the curved inner wall of the well was missing. He climbed through the hole, toward the flicker of Lepic's flashlight. On the other side of the opening was a low rough-hewn alcove where Lepic knelt beside the missing block of stone. Behind him, Gerd was climbing down a ladder into another hole.

Jarrell helped Lepic lift the stone block. It was difficult, without being able to straighten from their kneeling position. But they managed to get it firmly back into place, blocking the opening to the well. Crawling to the other hole, Lepic led the way down the ladder.

By now Jarrell understood their direction. They were descending into a branch of the ancient water system running under the city; a subterranean labyrinth fed by aqueducts that stretched underground for miles to reach Marrakesh.

At the bottom of the ladder they entered a big tunnel, half filled with running water. It disappeared into utter darkness to the left and right. The surface of the flowing water gleamed blackly in the glare of the flashlight. A large, flat-bottomed rowboat floated in it, tied to an iron ring sunk in a short ledge of rough stone that served as a sort of dock.

There were no seats in the boat. The boxes had been laid in the bottom. The two biggest men, Josal and Chalker, sat on them holding the oars ready. Nora and Ali were crowded down in the back half of the boat with Venturi and Rosen. Lepic and Gerd got in the bow, settling down carefully so they wouldn't tip the boat. Jarrell cast off and squeezed in with them, just as carefully. It was a tight fit for all of them. Under the combined weight the boat sank almost to the gunwales; but not quite.

Lepic shone his light to the left, quietly giving directions as Chalker and Josal rowed. The boat glided smoothly under the arched walls, went around a tight bend, and entered a smaller tunnel from which even smaller ones branched off in different directions. Lepic turned them into one of these, and from that into others; following an intricate route through a murky, long-forgotten network of narrowing, crumbling passages burrowing under the decaying roots of the city.

Jarrell gave Lepic a questioning look. "These pipes keep getting smaller. They should be getting bigger, if we're on our way out of the city."

"We're not; not yet. We can no longer reach the place where I arranged for the transport to wait for us. So first I have to make a call and change the rendezvous point."

Nora Devlin's laugh was just a little strained. "Don't tell me you've even got a telephone somewhere down here."

Lepic glanced back with an indulgent smile. "No, there is a way to a house whose owner will let me use her phone." He looked at Jarrell. "Lalla Tanina's place. I assume you know it."

A corner of Jarrell's mouth twitched. "I know it. I didn't know there was a way into it from down here."

"You'll see."

They continued to thread deeper into the watery maze, turning from one passage into another, until it would have been impossible for any of them but Lepic to find the way out. The tunnels became progressively more decrepit as the boat glided into a section where repair attempts had been given up years before as hopeless. In places, chunks of the wall and roof had caved into the water, almost blocking their way. Centuries earlier, futile efforts had been made to shore these up; the boat's passengers had to bend almost double to get their heads under low, slimy arches.

Lepic's flashlight began to dim while they were still finding their way through the claustrophobic maze. Lepic cursed softly. "I forgot spare batteries."

Jarrell looked at the darkness drawing in closer around the weakening light. "That better be all you forgot."

The flashlight had become steadily weaker by the time the boat came out of a long, narrow tunnel. They found themselves inside a cavernous cistern. It was like an underground lake. Their feeble beam illuminated only a little of the nearest surface; it had no effect on the darkness shrouding the other side and the high ceiling.

The boat was rowed to the right along the near wall. Jarrell sensed, rather than actually saw, a vague shape gliding past in another direction through the murk to their left. They were not the only ones using the subterranean irrigation system to avoid government hunters this night.

Lepic took them past the opening of a large water tunnel, and into a very cramped one. It quickly became too narrow for rowing. The oars were pulled in. After that they had to push with their hands against the walls on either side to keep the boat moving.

Lepic stopped the boat by seizing something that Jarrell couldn't make out at first in the dying glow of the flashlight. Then he saw that it was a dangling ladder of chains and iron bars. Lepic aimed the flashlight straight up. There was a circular hole in the vaulted roof above them, almost as wide across as the tunnel itself. The ladder ran up its blackness, where the flashlight beam could no longer reach. Jarrell judged it to be the bottom of a well-hole, once used to supply water to the house above by lowered buckets.

And sometimes for more macabre purposes. If that was Lalla Tanina's house up there, they were now under what had been the infamous "district of discarded wives," now a rabbit warren of native prostitution, in which Lalla Tanina's was the most elegant establishment. In the old days prostitutes had been known to drop the dead bodies of men they'd robbed and murdered through holes like the one above. They didn't do that any more, it was said. But the holes were still there.

Jarrell took the flashlight from Lepic. "Remember. Batteries."

Lepic shot him a hurt look and began climbing the

ladder, the jangling of the chains echoing unnervingly through the confines of the tunnel. He disappeared into the blackness of the well above. Jarrell listened for a knocking up there, but heard none. But there must have been some kind of signal device attached to the ladder itself. A circle of lantern light abruptly showed at the top of the well, darkly silhouetting Lepic, and the head and torso of someone bending over him.

Whispers rang down to the boat, distorted by the well. Then Lepic climbed up into the lantern light, which cut off abruptly as a trap door closed on the top of the well. Thirty seconds later, the flashlight went dead in Jarrell's hand, and they were plunged into a darkness so total they couldn't see each other; couldn't have seen a mirror two inches from their eyes.

For a time no one said anything. The darkness became a living presence, smelling of age, decay, and dripping malevolence. They sat in it listening to their own breathing, and the unseen water gurgling inches beneath them. And to the squealing of water rats, which rose to an echoing crescendo as the time stretched on.

Josal snapped on a cigarette lighter, his face contorted with loathing. Thousands of tiny eyes gleamed at them in its sudden flare, before fleeing from it into the surrounding shadows.

"I can't stand the vermin near me," Josal said thickly. He kept the lighter burning until it grew too hot to hold and he had to flick it off.

The darkness came back. And very quickly, the squealing was back, too. Josal snapped his lighter again, but it wouldn't catch. He kept trying, fruitlessly. A lighter flared in Venturi's thick fist, and the rats fled again. In the light, Josal's face had a sheen of sweat.

"I understand how you feel," Venturi muttered. "Once I spent two days hiding from the Germans under a barn. I still have scars where they tried to eat me."

Between Venturi and Nora, Ali was leaning against the wall with his eyes shut, as though trying to fall asleep to escape his terror. Nora struck a match and used it to light a cigarette, flicking the match away into the darkness. As it sizzled out in the water, Jarrell looked at her. The corners of her mouth had a pinched look. And she drew too hard at the cigarette. Otherwise, she didn't show any sign of having to hold onto her nerves. The girl had guts. But he'd already known that.

It seemed like a long time. But Jarrell reckoned it at less than fifteen minutes before the circle of light at the top of the well flowed down over them again. Lepic descended the ladder, stepping carefully into the overloaded boat. He drew a long three-battery flashlight from his robes. The trapdoor above closed down as he snapped it on.

Jarrell slit his eyes against the sudden glare. "You put the call through?"

Lepic nodded. "The truck'll be waiting for us."

"Then let's get the hell out of here."

The end of the line was in a well-tended main inflow tunnel. The current there of the water piped in from the distant rivers was so strong they had trouble rowing against it, though they took turns at the oars. It was a relief when Mahjoub Lepic finally tied the boat securely to steel wall-rungs that had seen some recent use. The rungs led up through a repair hole used by workmen who kept the main irrigation lines functioning. The heavy grate across the top had no securing lock on it. Jarrell shoved it up and aside, and climbed out of the hole with the AR ready in one hand and set to full automatic fire, just in case.

He looked around swiftly as the others came up. They were several miles outside Marrakesh, deep in the date-palm forest that surrounded it.

There was a truck parked in the night shadows of the trees twenty yards away. It had an old-fashioned Chevrolet chassis, with a high front cab, and a rounded dome of patched black canvas covering the cargo-carrying section in back of the cab. Jarrell waited until Gerd came up from the hole with his repeating shotgun. Then they advanced on the truck, circling to either side of it.

The truck was empty, as it was supposed to be. No one

in sight around it. Chalker strode over with his M-16 in his hands and his .38 in a belt holster, followed closely by Josal with a Schmeisser machine-pistol and Luger. Jarrell sent them to scout through the surrounding trees. Far enough to warn of approaching trouble in time; near enough to get in fast when it was time to go.

Inside the back of the truck were filled water canteens and packs bulging with food and supplies. Plus spare packs, into which they distributed the ammo, grenades, and explosives from the boxes. The cork-padded pack containing the precious wireless transmitter was carefully placed among these inside the truck. Jarrell apportioned the rest of the weapons, along with commando knives.

He gave a second repeating shotgun to Lepic, who had his own handgun, a Webly automatic. Marcel Venturi, in addition to his .45, got Chalker's M3, the tough and inelegant lightweight submachine gun the U.S. Marines called a "grease gun." For Rosen, a long-ranging Garand rifle, and a snub-nosed .38 Colt Cobra revolver, in case he had to defend himself at close quarters.

Ali began to look a good deal more sure of himself once he had an M–1 carbine gripped firmly in his hands. Until that moment, Jarrell figured, Ali hadn't been completely sure if he was really one of the team, or its prisoner.

Jarrell offered Nora a small Beretta pistol she could easily hide inside her *djellabah*. "You never know, could be a time you'll need it."

She shook her head firmly. "It's not my kind of weapon, Jarrell. I don't know how to use it, and I don't want to."

He accepted that. People who carried guns they didn't know how to use were more danger to themselves than to anyone else. And there was no time left to teach her. Anyway, she was right: Fending off trouble was his job, not hers.

Gerd had already chosen an extra weapon, in addition to the shotgun and thirteen-round Browning H-P pistol: a .303 Lee Enfield rifle with an effective range of two thousand yards, with a telescope sight that could be attached to it in just over one second by an expert, making it as good a sniper's weapon as Rosen's Garand.

"You go in front with Lepic and me," Jarrell told him. "Everybody else in back, with Marcel in charge there."

Marcel Venturi pulled aside the canvas flap and led the way up inside the back of the truck. Jarrell headed for the cab, noting with approval that the heavy-tread mud tires were in good condition. The rest of the truck looked pretty beat up; which would make it no different from a lot of other freight and farm-produce trucks on the road, so they shouldn't attract undue attention. If they attracted it anyway, they'd just have to handle it.

He climbed in behind the wheel, with Lepic between him and Gerd. The motor started smoothly, sounding a lot newer than the rest of the truck. The sound brought Chalker and Josal out of the trees .on the run. They scrambled in back as the truck got moving, following a path through the trees under Lepic's directions.

A few minutes later they were out of the palm forest, speeding along a good road that cut straight to the south. Thirty-five miles ahead of them, the seemingly endless bulk of the Atlas Mountains was still engulfed in night. But the highest peaks already glowed with the angry flame of approaching dawn.

NINE

It looked like two columns of black smoke. They rose into the glare of the sun from behind one of the broken ridges in the distance. Jarrell tooled the truck out of a stony ravine onto a better vantage point. Only one of the dark columns was rising smoke.

The other was descending—thousands of vultures, kites and ravens, homing in on the scent of death.

A battle had been fought up there this morning. It was over; or the carrion birds would still be hovering. Jarrell understood now the lack of any traffic that had worried him all morning.

They'd gone off the main road into the mountains with the full light of dawn, taking unpaved paths to lower the chance of running into an official road block. Even so, it would have been normal to see *some* other movement along the route they were following. What had happened up there behind that ridge, under those two dark columns, explained why there'd been none. All the government vehicles in the area were up there, involved in it. And all other vehicles were carefully staying well clear of the area.

Which was a sensible idea. Except that this was the way to get where they were going, in time for getting there to mean anything.

"How close can we get to the village with this truck?" Gerd asked Lepic.

102

"We'll have to climb about the last ten miles on foot."

Jarrell nodded at the dark columns. "Unless *that* was our village."

The corners of Lepic's sardonic mouth stretched a bit as he studied landmarks and estimated distances. "It's quite possible."

Jarrell put that problem aside for when and if they got to it. What concerned him at the moment was getting off the side of this barren slope, on which there was no concealing cover. The truck could be clearly spotted from any of the surrounding ridges for miles around.

He concentrated on pushing the truck up a steep, narrow ledge rising over a sheer drop.

The air was so sharp at this height that mind and instinct seemed to operate with abnormal clarity. They were well above the bulky folds of the foothills; into a different world. A desolate, forbidding world of glaring stone that loomed into the sky all around them, clawed into tormented shapes by the winds, rains, and erosion of eternity. The truck crawled through it like a beetle lost in a weird moonscape.

Below, the chasm whose side it was climbing dropped into murky depths. Above, gigantic, sharp-toothed peaks lifted raggedly out of bulging cliffs that overhung the truck, pressing down with crushing weight. They were utterly cut off from even a hint of Marrakesh and its plain in one direction; of the limitless wastes of the Sahara in all other directions.

Occasionally, there was a glimpse of green—a patch where a tiny farm had been scratched out of a meager ledge—a sliver where a mountain stream cut its way down. But most of the time there was only naked stone, dust, and barren clay. And enormous silence.

They were entering the Zone of Insecurity. That was the official name. An older name clung to it: *bled es siba*—country without law. One look at it explained why. Just a few miles higher, the terrain became impassable for tanks, trucks, or any kind of vehicle. The government's struggle to conquer the lawless clans up in there had to be conducted without modern heavy armor. There *was* a way

103

to get troops in quickly: by helicopter. But once they were down on the ground, the only ways left to move in any direction from the landing point were by horse or mule, or on foot. In ambush country known intimately by the warriors they were sent to find and fight.

The kind of men that Jarrell knew were watching the truck's movements through their territory now, though he couldn't spot any of them. It was impossible for them not to be aware of its presence. In that vast silence, the sound of a truck would echo for miles. If it weren't for the increasing pressure of time, Jarrell would have left the truck where they were, and continued on foot. But the pressure was there.

Jarrell got the truck over the crest of the slope, and headed down the other side. They were into another chasm; one side of it white rocks reflecting the direct glare of the sun, the other side in dark purplish shadow. This time they were on the shadowed side, where the truck could no longer be seen from a distance; though it was still just as easy to hear.

The route Jarrell followed clung to the slope, snaking toward the notch of a high pass through barriers of uprearing brown rock. The chasm narrowed into a canyon formed by a long-vanished river that had denuded the slopes of soil. In spite of the steepness of their shadowed slope, it was easy for Jarrell to keep the truck on the track leading to the pass. Centuries of travelers had sunk the path below the ground on either side of it. This was one of the ancient routes of caravans that had carried gold and slaves all the way up from Timbuktu.

As they got nearer, they could make out two fortress villages that had once controlled the pass; built high into the opposite slopes. Both were now fire-blackened ruins, their mud defense walls collapsing, only crumbling remnants of their once-formidable square towers left.

Jarrell eyed them distrustfully. "Have to check them out, before we go through under them."

"Those castles have been empty for years," Lepic told him.

Jarrell nodded. "That doesn't say they're empty *now*."

"Mud returning to mud," Gerd murmured. "What happened up there—the army finally take them?"

"Not the army," Lepic said. "They took each other. Two brothers ruled in them; one in each. Their grandfather had seized the pass and gotten rich making anyone who used it pay toll. Their father built the two castles, and got richer. The brothers inherited the castles, and fought to the death over which should get all the riches." The sardonic twist of Lepic's mouth got more pronounced. "There are hundreds of these ruins in the Atlas. In Morocco, nothing lasts more than three genera——"

The rest of what he had to say was cut short by Chalker calling sharply through the small window connecting the cab to the rear of the truck. "Jarrell—there's a chopper coming in behind us!"

Jarrell stamped down on the foot brake, cut the motor, and set the hand brake—all within seconds. With the truck standing still in deep shadow, a helicopter wasn't likely to spot it unless it came down very low. In the next second he was out of the truck looking up and back.

The helicopter was coming from the northwest, flying just high enough to suit Jarrell. He raised and focused the field glasses hanging on a thong around his neck. It was a big CH-47 Chinook, capable of airlifting up to forty-three fully equipped troops, or twenty-thousand pounds of heavy guns and ammo. And there were three more of the same coming up behind it from the same direction. Heading for the dark columns of smoke and birds of prey. So whatever was happening up there was still going on.

Jarrell lowered the glasses and ordered everybody out of the truck to stretch their legs. He watched the big Chinooks fly over them, the thunder of their motors reverberating down into the canyon. When the last one vanished over the pass, he looked back where they'd come from.

Nothing else was there. Jarrell waited, and after a while there was something. Just a dark speck moving against the sky.

Jarrell used the glasses again. It was a little observation

chopper. An OH-6 Cayuse, coming in slowly, and very low. As it got over the other end of the canyon it began circling; lower and lower.

There was nothing to do about that but wait it out; and trust to the slope's shadow to go on concealing the motionless truck.

"We'll be here a bit," Jarrell announced as he let the glasses drop at the end of their thong.

He sent Chalker up to check out one of the fortress ruins siding the pass; Gerd to the other. That had to be done anyway. It might as well be taken care of during the forced wait. He didn't tell them to keep to cover all the way; nor what to do if they detected trouble waiting in the ruins. If they'd needed telling, he wouldn't have chosen them.

To Josal he assigned the job of keeping watch on the spotter plane's movements. If it came in close enough to spot them, they were going to have to try shooting it down.

Getting a thickly folded map from the cab of the truck, Jarrell called Ali and Mahjoub Lepic. As he hunched down and unfolded the map on a flat rock, he noticed that Nora Devlin was already sitting on the ground against the rear wheel of the truck, swiftly scribbling notes in her pad. Doing her job; as he was tending to his. The difference being that hers had a future, while his future was just about played out for him.

After this one last time.

The map was the most detailed one Lepic could get of the area they were in. "Show me the village where we find your contact," Jarrell told Ali. "In relation to where we are now."

Ali scowled uncertainly over the map. Lepic helped him pick out the two spots on it: where they were, and where they were going. Jarrell scrutinized the layout of the terrain in between. Then he glanced up to where the dark columns still showed, though more faintly in a sky getting hazy with cloud mists drifting up there.

If the village with Ali's contact wasn't the one burning, it had to be pretty close to it. Which meant they were going to have to slip in through government troops; maybe run from them. He asked Ali to tell him everything he could remember about the terrain around his contact's village, and listened carefully to what Ali had to say, locating each point on the map.

Then he moved the tip of one finger in a semicircle on the map, in the area above and behind the contact's village. "Bel Zaara should be somewhere in there, according to the time it took your man from the village to take Nora Devlin to him. What's the country like back up in there?"

Ali shook his head. "I do not know it. I have only been as far as my friend's village."

"*I've* been up through there," Lepic said, studying the map. "Once I even had to hide in a cave network I found in there, for two days. An affair with some brigands. But it turned out well. I found some neolithic carvings and wall paintings while I was hiding. Sold them later for a very good price, to a museum. I even found some dinosaur tracks nearby; unfortunately impossible to remove for sale. It is very old country."

"Tell me about it," Jarrell said.

He concentrated on the map while soaking up everything he was told.

The helicopter was circling over the opposite side of the canyon now, where sunlight banished shadows and showed everything starkly. Josal leaned against the rear of the truck, his big figure looking relaxed but his expressionless eyes never leaving the chopper.

Rosen was watching it, too; the strain showing on him. "What the hell is it *staying* here for?"

Marcel Venturi put a thick arm around Rosen's shoulders. "Don't worry, my friend. It will have to leave. It will run out of petrol. Then we can go on. Try to relax."

"That's easy to say." Rosen's voice was an agonized whisper. "That's my daughter they've got somewhere up there. And her mother."

"No," Venturi corrected gravely, "it is not easy for me to tell you to relax. I know they hold women who are precious to you. But *we* have my friend Jarrell to lead us. He will get them out safely, depend on it."

Nora Devlin looked up from her notepad, caught by the old-fashioned dignity with which he had pronounced this. "You're very confident of what your friend Jarrell can do."

Venturi turned his head and looked at her coolly for a moment, until he was certain she was neither mocking nor challenging him. "I am," he told her quietly. "My friend Jarrell is a very special kind of man. As you will learn. I believe in him. If you do not, you should not be here with us. Because all our lives, including yours, depend upon this man."

"You talk as though everything hangs on just one man. What about the rest of you?"

"We are just his soldiers," Venturi told her.

Rosen was deep in his troubled thoughts, listening to none of this. "And what happens if we do get to this village, and the man there *won't* take us to where they're hidden?"

Josal gave a short, harsh laugh, without taking his attention off the circling helicopter. "Then you will give him to me. For about fifteen minutes; no longer. He will tell us everything we want to know."

Nora closed her notebook and got to her feet, looking at Josal. Especially the brutality of the mouth. "You sound as though you've tortured men before."

Josal smiled a little. "I have. And women, too. But," he added, "only bad people, with whom it was necessary. Very bad people."

"Did you *enjoy* it?"

Josal's smile slowly crumpled. Something frightened came into his face. After a moment he whispered, "Yes. I did enjoy it."

He crossed himself quickly as he said it. Nora was sure he didn't know he had done that. She moved away from him. *Had* to move away from him; as from someone with a loathsome disease.

She turned from the truck and looked toward Jarrell, who was folding the map as he rose to his feet. He glanced first toward the hovering chopper, then at the ruins on each side of the pass; where Chalker and Gerd were, though they could not be seen. He continued to look, waiting.

Nora studied him, thinking about what Venturi had said.

Josal called out softly: "She's going . . ."

Everyone turned to look. The helicopter was rising into the sky, heading on over the pass.

When Nora looked at Jarrell again, he was once more watching the ruins Gerd and Chalker were scouting. He was standing perfectly still, watching an area that hid two of his men. But there was a high-voltage electricity to him that could be *felt*. Like a quiet powerhouse just waiting for something to throw the switch.

Nora wondered if it was because she was trying to look at him through Marcel Venturi's eyes. She hadn't seen this Jarrell before. It came to her that she *was* watching something very special. Something she hadn't come across even in Vietnam, where she'd seen some damn good officers in action.

And he wasn't in action.

Just standing there.

Curiosity, or the electricity, drew her over to him. He knew she was there, but he didn't take his attention off the pass; even while she told him what Josal had said.

"I was just wondering about it—*would* you give a man to Josal to torture?"

"No."

"You do have scruples. Interesting."

"It wouldn't be practical. He might tell us an opposite direction." He still wasn't looking at her. She knew it was just one small part of him that was answering her. The rest of him was up there with his unseen men. "By the time we'd found out he was lying, and Josal worked on him again, we could be too far to get back there in time."

"Whatever you do has to have a practical reason, is that it?"

"In my work, yes. Is there another way?"

Nora shook her head slowly. "You *are* a good officer, I'll give you that."

But none of him was with her any longer. "Gerd's coming down."

Nora looked up at the pass, but she couldn't see Gerd. He was coming though; she knew that by Jarrell's profile. He'd relaxed a notch; just a notch. Now all his attention was on the ruins that concealed Chalker. She looked again at the slope below the ruins that Gerd had been investigating. Finally she caught a glimpse of him, as he slid down a steep incline between two boulders with his feet spread like a skier, all of his athletic figure perfectly balanced.

Jarrell said suddenly: "And there's Chalker."

The way he said it made Nora look at him first, rather than at the pass.

All the electric tension was gone. Completely. He looked almost sleepy.

And then he stopped looking sleepy. "He's not coming down."

Nora looked up at the pass then. It took a few moments for her to locate Chalker, small in the distance. He stood on top of a ruined tower, raising his rifle above his head; making signals with it.

Jarrell focused his field glasses on him. "Get everybody ready to go to work," he told Nora.

"What is it?"

Jarrell continued to read Chalker's signals through the glasses.

"Trouble," he answered in a dead-level voice. "We're in trouble."

TEN

The army road block on the other side of the pass consisted of two open Land Rovers and a canvas-topped jeep equipped with a two-way radio-phone, whose long antenna stuck up from beside the windshield. There were six troopers to each Land Rover, armed with the latest FN automatic rifles. The officer in charge of the road block, a lieutenant of the Royal Moroccan Army, had the radio jeep, with a driver and two troopers carrying submachine guns.

Everything about the road block was exactly as it should be, considering the terrain. The two Land Rovers made a barrier across the width of the road, one facing the pass, the second facing the other way, to where the road cut into another canyon. The officer's jeep faced the road on the left side, blocking the narrow open space between the road and the bottom of a steep cliff from which jagged formations jutted like huge black teeth.

There was much more open space on the other side of the road, where the ground sloped up gently for some distance to the boulder-strewn base of another rugged cliff. A vehicle could try swinging around the road block through this open area. But it wouldn't get far before getting trapped between the Land Rovers circling in on it from opposite directions and the jeep cutting in between.

A perfect road block, in every way except one: It had been there since dawn, and not a single vehicle had come along the road in either direction all day. It was now mid-afternoon. The men were getting bored and sleepy under the hot dazzle of the sun. Even their officer didn't spot the four men coming along the road toward the block until they were out of the shadowed pass.

Four armed men, coming on foot. If their appearance was unexpected, they seemed just as surprised to find the road block there. They stopped dead, staring at it. Then they broke and ran. Chalker, the man in the lead, sprinted along the boulder-strewn cliff base that curved around the gradually rising ground on the right side of the road. Lepic, Ali, and Josal raced after him.

The men at the road block broke out of their own surprise. The Land Rover drivers scrambled in and started the motors as their lieutenant barked the order. They took off as soon as all their men had piled in, churning up clouds of dust as they roared across the long open rise.

The jeep stayed where it was, with the driver ready behind the wheel and the motor running in neutral; in case anyone else came along the road. The lieutenant stood beside the jeep with its two troopers, watching the Land Rovers close in on the fleeing men.

The four men vanished, in among the boulders at the base of the distant cliff. Then one or another of them appeared briefly. They were climbing the narrow gullies that cut down the rugged face of the cliff.

The Land Rovers skidded to a halt at the barrier of the boulders. Troopers leaped out, automatic weapons ready in their hands. The four climbing men could no longer be seen to shoot at, among the shadowed formations and fissures above. The troopers headed into the boulders after them; twelve men against four. It was going to be an exciting hunt. Their lieutenant, watching from the road, was pleased with the way they fanned out before starting to climb. Good soldiers; well trained.

A canvas-backed truck came speeding out of the pass.

This time what was left of the road block was not caught by surprise. The two troopers instantly unslung their submachine guns and leveled them. The lieutenant drew his holstered pistol and signaled the truck to stop.

112

Obediently, the truck slowed down as it approached. The lieutenant saw that the driver was alone in the front seat. That didn't say what might be under the patched black canvas covering in back. The lieutenant snapped an order. One of his troopers dashed across the road to flank the slowly nearing truck. The other stayed with his officer.

Marcel Venturi brought the truck to a full stop. He kept his hands on the steering wheel and an anxious frown on his face as they approached him. Officer and trooper on one side; the second trooper on the other side.

They stopped and twisted to stare off up the long, rising open expanse, as the sound of an explosion reached them.

The four fleeing men hidden in the broken heights of the cliff had stopped fleeing. They were tossing out hand grenades, bouncing them down at the troopers below them. A second grenade exploded among them as they stopped climbing. When a third came bouncing their way, they began a wild scramble to get back down to the cover of the boulders, flinging themselves flat between them.

Beside the road, the lieutenant cursed, softly and viciously.

Jarrell eased from a shadowed cleft in the rocks, above and behind the jeep, and dropped the rest of the way. He hit the ground with his feet spread and his knees bent, the stubby AR submachine gun in his lean hands ready to swing in either direction.

He said it loud and fast: "Drop your weapons. Or die. Your choice."

The jeep driver went rigid with his hands frozen to the steering wheel. His lieutenant and the two troopers started to twist around toward the sound of the voice. But then too many other things happened at the same time. Gerd and Rosen dropped from the back of the truck and stepped to either side of it, each aiming a rifle at a trooper. Venturi scooped the grease gun off his lap and poked it through the side window in the lieutenant's face. A short warning burst from Jarrell's AR chewed up fountains of dirt from one side of the road to the other, inches from their feet.

The trooper beside the lieutenant tried to finish his turn, with his submachine gun up in firing position. He didn't quite make it. Rosen's heavy Garand blasted his shoulder apart. The impact at that short range spun him in the air before sprawling him on the ground. His submachine gun fell in the middle of the road.

Jarrell's voice was quieter this time: "I did say drop them."

Venturi smiled coldly down the short length of the grease gun. The lieutenant's fingers seemed to spring open of themselves, the pistol falling from them. The trooper on the other side of the road looked down Gerd's rifle to the finger poised across the trigger. It became very clear to him that even if he could nail Gerd with a burst before that trigger squeezed, Jarrell's AR would rip his head off before he could make the full turn for a second burst. He dropped his gun, and raised both arms as high as he could.

Jarrell looked toward the cliff where Chalker was in charge. It had been quiet there for a few seconds. Troopers began rising up cautiously among the boulders for a look at what was happening at the road. Instantly, two live grenades came lobbing down at them from Chalker's hidden squad.

The troopers dropped out of sight in the protection of the boulders. No more grenades fell. The lesson was obvious. As long as they stayed flat where they were, no grenades. But that way they couldn't get up the cliff, or back to their Land Rovers.

Jarrell didn't want to give them time to figure a way out of that problem. He yanked the driver out of the jeep, making sure he didn't have a weapon on him. Nora Devlin climbed from the back of the truck.

"Gather up their guns," Jarrell told her, "and toss them in the truck." As she obeyed, he turned to the officer. "Walk into the pass back there. Quickly."

The lieutenant was studying him bleakly, fighting his fear. "Who *are* you?"

"That doesn't matter, lieutenant. What matters is that the rifles these two men are holding are the best long-range sniper's weapons available. If you slow down anywhere before you're inside that pass, they're going to shoot you. Dead." Rosen and Gerd raised their rifles just a bit, to drive home the point.

The lieutenant hesitated. Jarrell had to give him that. But then he began walking away toward the pass; as fast as he could without running. Which was sensible, because he had no alternative. The wounded trooper was dragged after him by the driver and the other trooper.

Nora threw the last of the weapons in the back of the truck and climbed in. Gerd climbed up beside Venturi. Jarrell got behind the wheel of the jeep, letting out the hand brake. Rosen swung in beside him. The jeep shot across the road and sped straight toward the two Land Rovers standing empty near the boulders. Venturi drove the truck off at an angle, circling toward the cliff but keeping out of range of the trapped troopers' weapons. Beside him, Gerd was attaching the scope sight to his Lee-Enfield.

Jarrell made the ballistic calculation as he approached the Land Rovers and boulders at the base of the cliff. He stopped the jeep just beyond the accurate firing range of the enemy weapons.

But not beyond the range of a Garand. Rosen got out of the jeep and went down on one knee, aiming carefully. His first shot shredded the left front tire of one Rover. Jarrell looked off to the truck. It had stopped, and Gerd stood with his back braced against it, looking through the scope on his Lee-Enfield.

Rosen's Garand blasted again and blew open the Land Rover's rear tire. He shifted to the other Rover. A couple of automatic rifles poked out of a shadow between two boulders and began firing in the direction of the jeep. Some of the slugs chopped up dirt yards short of it. Others sang harmlessly overhead. Gerd slammed off two shots anyway; because there was always a chance one of the enemy slugs would get lucky. The Lee-Enfield bullets slashed showers of rock splinters from the shadow between the boulders. One rifle yanked back out of sight and the other fell out of the shadow and lay there.

Rosen shot out the tires of the second Land Rover. Jarrell looked at the top of the cliff. Chalker appeared between two formations, climbing over a jut of stone to reach the rim. A trooper rose among the boulders, enough to take aim at Chalker. Gerd's Lee-Enfield sang out again. The trooper fell with a dangling arm, his automatic rifle bouncing away in the boulders. None of the other troopers rose up for another attempt. Chalker went over the rim, followed by Ali, Lepic, and Josal.

"The engines now," Jarrell told Rosen, who was reloading the Garand.

Rosen proceeded to make metal hash out of the Rover engines; then reloaded again. After that they just waited. Gerd put a shot into the boulders from time to time, just to keep the enemy pinned. Chalker reappeared, leading his squad down the cliff toward the truck.

Jarrell called Rosen back into the jeep. They joined up with the truck back at the road. While Rosen climbed in back with the others, Jarrell used a full magazine from the AR to destroy the jeep's radio, tires, and motor. Then he swung up in front with Venturi and Lepic.

The truck surged forward with a roar. Venturi headed it all-out into the next canyon, higher up. He was one of the best emergency drivers Jarrell knew; so Jarrell left that to him and their route to Lepic. He had a hard decision to make.

The chance of running into another road block increased as they penetrated deeper into territory where the fighting was going on. And the next one might catch *them* by surprise. The logical thing was to abandon the truck, soon; and continue on foot under low visibility conditions, away from the road. That would be safest, for them. But not for Rosen's daughter and ex-wife; because it would be a hell of a lot slower. And getting them out on time was what this paramilitary expedition was all about.

Jarrell turned his head and spoke through the window to those in the back of the truck: "Gather up all the stuff; packs, weapons, supplies, everything. Be set to hit the dirt with all of it when we run into trouble. And Chalker, I want two packs of dynamite ready. Short fuse on one; long on the other."

He'd opted for speed; which meant sticking with the truck as long as they could. Objectives dictated tactical decisions. That made this the right one; in spite of what they ran into an hour later.

ELEVEN

The truck had just turned into a very wide, high canyon when they spotted the next road block, in the distance ahead of them. And were spotted by it.

This one included a forty-six-ton JAGD-Panther tank.

Venturi jammed on the brakes and cursed. The tank, and three jeep-loads of troops, were lined up across the road in the middle of the canyon. Jarrell's face showed nothing but alert calculation as he did a fast scan.

From the road, the ground sloped up unevenly towards cliffs on either side; one brown, the other ebony. There was very little cover on either slope. Jarrell estimated their chance of swinging around the road block to get back on the road beyond it as nil. That old Panther's 88-mm cannon would blow the truck to splinters before they could get past. Jarrell gestured off to the right, where rising folds of lava rock rolled toward the top of the cliff like frozen black waves, cut through with ravines.

"Is there a way out up there?" he asked Lepic. Each word came out fast and sharp.

"Yes, but only on foot."

"That's the idea. Hit it, Marcel."

Venturi spun the truck off the road in a swirling cloud of dust. Jarrell leaned out the window to look back as it jounced wildly up the uneven ground. The jeeps started after them as the last troopers piled in. A moment later, so did the tank.

"Start dodging," Jarrell instructed Venturi. "Long, fast swings. Nothing they can predict."

Venturi began zigzagging the truck erratically in and out of the rocks scattered on the slope, like a daredevil stunt driver, spinning the wheel and skidding recklessly to send up as much of a dust screen as possible behind them.

"The jeeps will catch up quicker this way!" Lepic shouted above the noise of the truck.

"That *tank* is our first worry." Jarrell squinted back through the dust and past the fast-closing jeeps. The tank was lumbering up the slope, its big gun swinging from side to side trying to get a bead on the truck. But unable to because of Venturi's display of crazy driving.

The surplus JAGD-Panthers from World War II were still good tanks, in certain situations. But because they didn't have revolving turrets, the traversing arc of the cannon was strictly limited. The whole tank had to be swung around to aim the gun at a drastically different angle. The Panther's speed when new had been only thirty miles per hour. Even reconditioned, Jarrell doubted it could do more than twenty-five now. As long as Venturi kept the truck a wildly shifting target, the odds were against the Panther hitting it.

But the jeeps were getting too damn close.

Jarrell pulled in his head and studied the lava formations rising against the cliff ahead. "There's a deep ravine up there on the left. Get into it, fast. No more dodging."

Venturi spun the truck in that direction, its motor straining to churn it up the steepening slope. The booming of the Panther's cannon shook the air. The shell whined high over the truck and smashed lava rock into a cloud of black dust.

"Keep straight," Jarrell snapped to Venturi. It would take at least three shots for the tank to get their range. He turned and rapped orders into the back of the truck. Through the canvas flapping from the rear, he saw the jeeps still gaining on them. "Chalker, hit 'em with the short fuse."

Chalker brought up a cigarette lighter. He waited, gauging the distance. The lead jeep came close. Chalker lit the short fuse and tossed the small dynamite pack. It bounced directly in the jeep's path. The jeep swung away wildly, and crashed into a boulder, bending one front wheel out of shape. The troopers hurled themselves out of it on the far side, falling behind its cover as the explosion sent up a geyser of smoke and dust.

The two remaining jeeps swerved away. And then, as the dust and smoke settled, they came on after the truck again. But more cautiously and slowly.

The Panther's cannon boomed again. The shell rocketed past the truck. Down to the right level now; but too far to the side. Venturi tried to shove the gas pedal through the floor. The truck jolted over rocks and ruts with its motor screaming in protest. The next shot from the tank came close.

Venturi twisted the wheel. The truck skidded into the deep mouth of the ravine, churned up inside it with the right side scraping the stone wall, and jerked to a stop.

They were in the tight cover of the ravine now, but that was all. The way ahead was too narrow for anything but men afoot. Venturi kicked the left door open and jumped down. The others, loaded down with packs and weapons, were crowding up from the rear as Jarrell followed Lepic out. Lepic and Venturi grabbed their packs from Josal and Ali, and Lepic led them up through the ravine. Nora shot Jarrell a tight, anxious look as she hurried past after them. Chalker brought up the rear. Jarrell took the long-fused dynamite from him and joined Rosen and Gerd at the rear of the truck.

"Stop the jeeps," he told Gerd. He looked to Rosen as Gerd slung the shotgun over his shoulder and went down on one knee with the Lee-Enfield. "You pin the men down." Holding the small dynamite pack in one hand, Jarrell waited.

The first of the two surviving jeeps came into sight on the slope below the ravine entrance, surging up towards it.

Gerd fired two spaced shots. The jeep's left front tire blew out, sending it into a crazy skid that spun it completely around before flipping over on its side and dumping the troopers out.

None of them were hurt enough to stop them from picking up their weapons and dragging themselves to their feet. They started coming around the jeep. Rosen's Garand slammed out two fast shots, kicking a leg out from under one of them and knocking another over backward. The rest scrambled back down behind the cover of the overturned jeep.

The second jeep came up past it, more slowly. Gerd triggered one shot and popped the right front tire. The jeep skidded, but not so wildly. It came to a stop still upright. Some of its troopers moved to man the heavy machine gun rivet-mounted on it. They dropped that notion when Gerd and Rosen began snapping shots into them, and got behind the cover of their jeep as the others had done.

Waiting for the JAGD-Panther tank to come up.

"Time to go." Jarrell followed Rosen and Gerd past the side of the truck. He paused at the cab, lit the long fuse, and tossed the dynamite in. Then he charged up the ravine after the others. He was around a tight bend and had them in sight ahead, when the dynamite exploded behind him.

The explosion, and the wreckage of the truck, wouldn't delay the pursuers more than half a minute. But even that could be vital in giving them the slip. The ravine was narrow enough to hold off a pursuing army. But that meant taking the time to do it. Time that was passing for the women hostages, too. They had to keep moving; without anybody at their heels.

Jarrell caught up to the others as Lepic turned them out of the ravine, into another that went level for a short distance and seemed to dead-end against the black cliff. Not until they reached it could they see that there was a way through: a deep slit of a corridor, cutting straight between high black walls with big white knobs of salt cropping out of them.

Jarrell assigned Chalker and Josel to rear-guard, and

unslung his submachine gun as he joined Lepic in the lead. Gerd tagged close behind him, hanging the Lee-Enfield on his shoulder and unslinging the repeating shotgun. A long-range rifle would be no use at all in these close quarters.

The corridor took them through the cliff, into a bowl of red rock surrounded by crumbling yellow cliffs almost blocking out the sky. On the other side was a second corridor. This one led out to a large open space boxed in by sheer, marble-veined walls. It was filled with rainbow-sparkling spray from a waterfall plunging over a cut at the top of one cliff wall, and thundering past them down into a bottom hole in another.

Lepic led them around the wall and in behind the waterfall. Behind the pouring water was a cave. Lepic got out his flashlight and shone it in. The cave led into the dark womb of the mountain.

"It goes all the way through," Lepic told Jarrell. "And it is the *only* way through. Unless they climb over the mountain, which will take them many hours."

Jarrell took six steps into the cave, examining the walls and low roof of the entrance. There were deep cracks in the rock there; exactly what he needed.

Chalker had the pack with the explosives. Jarrell traded with him, and sent him deeper into the cave with Lepic and the others. Except Gerd, and Josal with his Schmeisser machine pistol. There wasn't room just inside the mouth of the cave for more than the two of them. They watched the water falling past and waited, ready to stop anyone trying to come in after them.

Crouching over Chalker's pack, Jarrell got out a small chunk of plastic explosive, plus adhesive tape and a pointed hammer. He had to stand on his toes to chop at the largest crack in the roof of the cave entrance with the pointed end of the hammer, deepening and widening the crack with each blow. He had the job half done when a trooper eased in under the waterfall, with his automatic rifle in firing position.

The thunder of Gerd's shotgun was deafening in that tight space. The concentrated load of shot had no time to spread. All of it pounded into the trooper and flung him through the curtain of falling water like a torn rag struck by a hurricane.

The instant he vanished the answer came: automatic fire, from at least four weapons. Bullets splashed through the falling water from different directions, filling the cave entrance with flying splinters of rock. Josal pressed against his side of the entrance and fired a full burst back through the waterfall, swinging the low-held Schmeisser in a tight arc to fling the bullets over a maximum range out there. The sound of an agonized cry came dimly through the noise of rushing water. The enemy fire ceased. Josal's brutal mouth smiled, but not his eyes. He began quickly reloading. Jarrell went on chopping at the crack in the stone above him. He had never stopped.

Another burst of slugs screamed into the cave entrance. One of them slashed through Josal's left upper arm and bounced off the stone behind him. He gasped, and sagged slightly. Then went on reloading, not backing away from the vulnerable spot. His teeth were bared in what could almost have been a smile of pleasure.

Gerd fired the rest of his shells through the waterfall, shifting the shotgun slightly between each blast. Jarrell, blood leaking from his cheek where a rock splinter had slashed him, stuck the hammer in his belt and stuffed the plastic explosive up into the enlarged crack. Josal sprayed another full burst at the unseen attackers while Gerd reloaded. The firing from outside stopped entirely. They were probably getting set to toss in grenades.

Jarrell fastened the explosive in place with two strips of tape, scooped up the pack, and slung it over one shoulder. "Now! Get out!"

Josal and Gerd went past him toward the interior of the cave. Jarrell lit the fuse and went after them in a fast crouch. He kept going through the murk until he came against a solid stone projection rising up from the cave floor. He swung around it and went down behind it.

The detonation one second later hammered his eardrums and lifted him a couple inches off the floor. The cave was filled with flying stones and choking dust. It took time for the concussion effect to clear from his brain. The dust was settling as he rose up for a look.

Lepic came up behind him and shone the flashlight toward the entrance. It was completely blocked with fallen rock. There was no way they'd be able to dig their way in through there in less than two days.

That didn't ease Jarrell's tension one bit. By now somebody around that road block would be in radio communication with wherever headquarters was. The people hunting them were going to have a lot of company to help in the hunt before long; coming from various directions.

When they emerged from the other end of the cave, some twenty minutes later, the first thing Jarrell did was look up at the sky, which was beginning to darken with the approach of dusk.

That was where the company would be coming from.

Allal Ben Hafidi, his gross bulk gorgeously attired in white silk *djellabah* and gold-embroidered blue *selham*, sat in a gilt and brocade chair in the midst of ancient ruins surrounded by ageless desolation. The column of smoke from the village the army had burned, and the column formed by the carrion birds, had been clearly visible from this place. Quite close, as the hawk flies. Though not for a man, because of the near-impassable ridges and gorges in between.

Traces of both columns still showed in the dimming light of evening. But Allal Ben Hafidi, seated between two bodyguards holding sharp swords with jeweled hilts, had no interest in them at this moment. Nor any thought for the female hostages entombed in the rock beneath his feet. His attention was on the line of horsemen coming out of the canyon and into the ruins.

He was aware that his nephew, Bel Zaara, was with them; returned at last. But he had eyes only for the first rider: a tall, slim youth with clear eyes and the pride of his heritage plain on his smooth face. Ben Hafidi's son, Hammou; only sixteen and already a warrior. More than that: a leader of warriors.

124

To Ben Hafidi's left, Colonel Omrani stopped his nervous pacing, waiting anxiously to hear the news the horsemen brought with them. The junior officers behind Omrani, men who had followed him here after the failure of their coup, were as tense as he. The strain of waiting here, while each day the army's search forces prowled closer, was showing on all of them.

Hammou reined his sturdy barb to a cruel and flashy halt, swinging down lightly from the crimson-clothed saddle. The boy hurried to bend a knee before his father, kissing his pudgy hands. Allal Ben Hafidi's disease-ravaged face flushed with pleasure. He took one of his son's slim hands in his own as the boy rose, smiling.

The voice of Bel Zaara, jumping down from his mountain horse, struck a jarring note: "I have met with my agents from Rabat. They say the government has no intention of releasing the hundred prisoners we listed as a condition for freeing our hostages."

Ben Hafidi frowned at him, absorbing this news. "The government has *said* this?"

"They do not *say* it. But it is so. I am as sorry to tell you this, my uncle, as you must be to hear it. But my agents are certain of it." Hastily, Bel Zaara added: "This can serve our purpose just as well. To make the government understand our seriousness. Killing the two women will force them to believe us, the next time."

"Then we might as well get it over with," Colonel Omrani growled. "Kill them now, and get away from here to a safer place."

Bel Zaara nodded, his hawk face tight with anger and disappointment. "There is no reason to wait any longer, now that we know."

Allal Ben Hafidi regarded Bel Zaara in silence for a moment. "My nephew," he reminded him sternly, "you gave our word that the hostages would not be killed until a certain time. That is soon; but not yet. We will wait. They will be killed at the promised time, in the proscribed manner."

Bel Zaara shrugged. "As you wish."

"Then take them with us," Colonel Omrani suggested

tensely. "The important thing is to get away from here. Before the army gets any closer."

Allal Ben Hafidi did not look at him. His eyes went to his young son. "Do they continue in this direction?"

Hammou grinned. "Not any longer. This is the news I came so quickly to bring you. Their main column walked into a trap el-Mansour set for them. His warriors slaughtered half their forces in the ambush. The other half are retreating to the west, through the Foum-el-Bali."

"They'll turn back," Colonel Omrani predicted heavily. "As soon as they are reinforced. And they *will* be reinforced."

Allal Ben Hafidi looked at him then. "We stay here," he said flatly. "No one can get in without being seen by my sentries. They will give us ample warning. These sentries are experienced warriors, with sharp eyes, who understand my orders." He paused, and then added pointedly: "Perhaps you should consider one of the orders I have given them. They will kill anyone who tries to leave this place before I give my permission."

Colonel Omrani forced himself to meet Ben Hafidi's stare. "I have no intention of doing so," he said stiffly. "I'll remain here as long as the rest of you do."

"Exactly," Allal Ben Hafidi said softly.

The sun was sinking into a deep notch between shadow-blackened peaks when the second big Chinook helicopter came in low overhead.

Jarrell, leading the way up a steep, loose-bottomed gully, called an instant halt. He glanced up at the rims of the eroded walls on either side, where Gerd and Chalker were flanking the gully on lookout. Both had already stopped moving, taking cover when they'd heard the chopper's approach.

Jarrell looked back down at the rest. The gully's darkness gave them ample cover. They were using the halt to settle down for a rest. He'd set a grueling pace, over hard, rising terrain. They were beginning to show the strain.

Not so much Ali and Lepic; they were used to this.

And Rosen still had plenty of stamina left; all that hunting and skiing had kept him in shape. But Nora had lost some of her youthful resilience. And Marcel Venturi was showing his age.

Santiso Josal, his arm bandage bulging under his sleeve and his face drawn from loss of blood, was in the worst shape. But he'd kept the pace Jarrell had set without complaint, his brutal mouth clamped stubbornly shut. Jarrell remembered Josal in the cave entrance. It was one of the paradoxes of battle that observers found hard to adjust to: Evil men could show guts like anybody else; or cowardice, like anybody else.

Jarrell looked again toward the troop-transport helicopter. It was lowering for a landing to the north, behind a ridge with ravines like deep black scars. The first Chinook they'd spotted, an hour back, had landed close to the south, on the other side of Jarrell's route. Each landing some forty troopers to join in the hunt for him.

Jarrell signaled the others to follow as he resumed the climb. At the top rose a grim black monolith, its ponderous bulk strangely intimidating as it merged into the darkening sky. Between it and the gully was a space of flat rock, protected on both sides by low, jagged ridges casting long evening shadows.

Between the peaks rising above, the sunset turned fat clouds crimson and purple, the cliffs silver and gold. But in ten minutes blackness would wipe out all color.

"We'll settle here for the night," Jarrell announced, signaling Chalker and Gerd to guard positions on the near ridges. He unslung his heavy pack and set it on the ground.

"We can reach that village tonight," Rosen protested.

Jarrell nodded. "But it'll be too dark. I don't intend to get near the village until we can see what we're going into. And we all need a night's sleep."

"I'm not that tired yet," Rosen persisted anxiously. He turned to Venturi. "What about you?"

Venturi smiled and shook his head. "We're a couple tough old roosters, eh?"

"I want you not tired when it *matters*," Jarrell said flatly. "Which will be tomorrow. Don't worry, we still have the time. But we've got to use it the right way. Tomorrow's going to be a hard day. And a long one."

Rosen contemplated Jarrell unhappily, thinking about it. Then he nodded, and joined the others in readying an evening meal. A cold one; with no fire to pinpoint their position.

Darkness was total by the time they finished. Jarrell sent Lepic to take over the first night watch from Gerd, and himself went up to relieve Chalker. Settling down on a high dome of fissured rock, he began picking out landmarks that emerging starlight revealed to the east. The direction they'd be taking with dawn.

One by one, he identified each landmark with some point on the map he'd memorized, going over tomorrow's terrain in his head. Considering every possible thing they could run into; settling on each countermove.

A slight sound made him raise the stubby submachine gun and twist around. It was Nora Devlin, coming up through the starlit darkness to him.

He lowered the AR. "We'll be starting at dawn. The longer you take to go to sleep, the less you'll get. And you'll need it tomorrow; that I guarantee."

She sat down on the rock dome with him. "Soon. I was just going over notes in my head. Fact's I still don't know about some of you. For example, why you quit the British army. I'd say you were a natural."

"I was. But then they sent me to North Ireland."

She studied his shadowed face. Neither its expression, nor his voice, told her anything she could read. "And being Irish, you didn't like the idea of killing Irishmen; or being killed by them. That it?"

"No. I'm only half Irish. The other half's French Canadian and Mohawk Indian. Neither half liked being a policeman when I'd signed on to be a soldier." His tone was lazy, uncaring. "I said so. Some people didn't like the way I said so. That's all there is to it."

"I see. Ever sorry about it?"

"No. You don't have to interview me. You already know all you want to know."

"Details help."

Jarrell grinned. "You mean colorful details. Like Chalker's harem."

Nora shrugged. "It helps to fill out the picture of what the man is."

He made an abrupt, impatient motion. "Does it? I don't think so. You think he's a man with too many girl-friends. I think that's only a way he relaxes. The *man* is the one who spotted that first road block for us; going up where he could get a strangler's cord around his neck or a knife in the back before he knew anybody was around him. And ready to do it again, as many times as it has to be done to get this job finished."

"That's one side of him. There are others."

"None that matter. Not to me. What a man *is*, is what he does under pressure. The way you go right on doing your job, even though you know you might be killed right in the middle of scribbling those notes of yours."

Nora had been looking at the stars, listening for nuances in his tone. Now her eyes slid back to him. "I guess that's meant to be a compliment to me, as a woman."

"No. As a reporter. As a woman, there's only one way to find out what you are. You know that. The same way you'd get to know a man who interested you enough to try it."

He was looking straight at her, but she still couldn't quite read him. She shook her head ruefully. "If there's one thing I've learned, Jarrell, it's that you can lie even in bed. You can *both* be lying."

Jarrell's smile was as dry as his voice. "Sure. But not for long. You get tired of the game, and the truth comes out."

This time there was an undertone of feeling she could identify. "Is that what happened to *your* marriage?"

"No. I just wasn't cut out for it. At least, not with a woman who didn't have anything else on her mind except her house, and me; in that order." Jarrell looked off

129

at the shadowed night to the east. It was a moment before he went on, carelessly: "I might have been better at it, with a woman who had something of her own. Like you."

Nora stared at him.

He laughed softly and looked at her again. "Don't let it scare you. It wasn't a proposition."

Her own laugh was a bit shaky. "It's just—My ex-husband *didn't* like my having my own thing. He wanted me to concentrate entirely on him and the apartment; in that order. I tell you, Jarrell, people are hard to figure."

"Sometimes. Some of them." He raised a hand from the submachine gun and closed it lightly around her arm. "Get to sleep now."

It was a flat command, and he let go of her arm as he said it. But she felt an odd little electric shock, where he'd touched her. She stood up, and went back down the slope without another word.

Jarrell returned his hand to the stubby AR and began restudying the landmarks to the east. Going over again each of the probabilities, possibilities, and countermoves.

A droning sound made him look up. The black outline of another Chinook moved across the stars. This one was flying to the east. Jarrell watched it go down for a landing.

There were only a few passes through the cliffs this high up. By morning there were going to be troops ambushing every one of them.

Tomorrow was going to be hell.

TWELVE

The hot sun radiated diffused red-gold light through purple-gray clouds between the mountain peaks. It revealed a land as nakedly hostile as a sword blade, concealing people to match. A chaos of disordered hills, jagged ridges, furrowed slopes, monstrous formations, broken canyons, and eroded ravines, with the massive ochre cliffs brooding over all.

A drop of salt slid down Jarrell's cheek past the side of his nose. The tip of his tongue flicked out and licked it away. Otherwise he remained perfectly still. His mouth was dry. But it wasn't thirst. It was what the field glasses showed him in the tight pass below.

He was belly down on a high lip of rock in the shadow of a lava overhang. It was the last patch of cover for three hundred yards, until the outcroppings on the other side. That completely exposed stretch of three hundred yards had to be crossed. It was the only way left to reach the other side of the pass. And the only way to reach the village from this point.

Hot perspiration oozed around the field glasses where he held them screwed to his eyes. He counted thirty-one troopers down there in the pass. The open stretch that had to be crossed was less than five hundred yards above the bottom of the pass. Within accurate range of the CAL assault rifles each of those troopers carried.

There was also a heavy-duty machine gun halfway up

the slope across from Jarrell, manned by two troopers and protected by piled rocks and sandbags. A similarly protected emplacement was halfway up the other slope, directly below Jarrell. This one contained a three-man team with a heavy mortar. Higher up on each side of the pass, almost exactly on a level with Jarrell's patch of concealing shade, was a sentry with binoculars.

But there was no other route.

Jarrell lowered the field glasses very slowly, so the sentries wouldn't be alerted by the movement within the overhang's shadow. His eyes slid to his wrist watch. Two minutes more. Jarrell licked another drop of sweat from his upper lip and waited. Two minutes can drag. The small of his back began to itch. Nerves. He stayed motionless, looking at the troops barring his way. His face became a sullen mask, but the eyes remained coldly calculating.

A rifle made a small sharp sound in the distance, more than one thousand yards beyond the other slope of the pass. One of the army sentries twisted and dropped, his rifle spilling into the pass below.

Even with a Lee-Enfield and a scope sight, there weren't many who could do that, at that distance. Gerd could. The second sentry spun to stare at the place where the first one had dropped. He was still staring when Gerd's second shot knocked him off his perch and sent him rolling down the slope.

The troopers in the bottom of the pass boiled into motion. Jarrell didn't move at all; just watched. Gerd's next two shots wiped out the pair at the heavy machine gun. One trooper started up to man it. A bullet from Gerd's hidden position ripped his arm and sent him scrambling back down to join the other ten already behind cover protecting them from Gerd's angle of fire. The rest of the troopers were following an officer up a gully in Gerd's direction.

Gerd kept snapping shots at them, shooting and reloading so fast it sounded like the fire of several rifles. None of these shots hit anyone. The officer, and the men following him, were keeping well down as they approached. Gerd stopped shooting. The troops working their way up toward his position continued their slow, cautious approach. Away from Jarrell's position; away from the open stretch that had to be crossed.

Jarrell's eyes slid to his watch again. He gave Gerd six minutes to get to him. That was something else not many could manage, from that far away over that kind of terrain, staying hidden all the way. Another reason Gerd had been his first choice for this expedition.

At five minutes, the officer and his troopers were almost up to the place Gerd had shot from. Well beyond effective range from the ledge where Jarrell lay. He looked into the pass below him, past the mortar emplacement. The cover the troopers had gotten behind shielded them from Gerd's original position; but not from Jarrell's. He raised and lowered one foot.

Chalker was the first to squirm up onto the lip of rock beside Jarrell. He put down a prepared and fused explosive pack, and moved on out of the patch of shadow, heading across the long open stretch as fast as he could on the steep slope. Lepic went past after Chalker without pausing. Then Ali, Nora, and Venturi. Josal was the last to go past Jarrell out into the open. His left fist was jammed down in his pocket so the wounded arm wouldn't swing and jolt him with pain. The Schmeisser was in his right, its aluminum-alloy stock folded for easier one-handed aiming and firing.

Rosen flopped down on the ledge beside Jarrell and aimed his Garand at the troopers crouched in the bottom of the pass. Jarrell waited with the explosive pack in one hand, cigarette lighter in the other.

Chalker, leading the others across the open stretch, had covered the first hundred yards when one of the troopers below looked up and saw them. Shouting a warning, the trooper twisted to fire up. Rosen's shot nailed him into the dirt. Jarrell lit the fuse and counted silently as the Garand kept blasting. The team with the mortar were getting it turned around. Rosen concentrated on the troopers at the bottom, making them scatter to other cover before they could stop to take aim at the group fleeing across the open space.

Jarrell tossed the pack, underhanded. The timing was right. It exploded exactly at the moment it landed inside the mortar emplacement; before any of the team could snatch it up and toss it away. No more mortar.

Rosen was reloading the Garand. In the lull, troopers began showing from behind their new cover to take aim. A slug chopped dirt from the slope between Venturi and Nora. Another slapped off the lava overhang above Jarrell's head. He snatched up the AR and raked long, slashing bursts into the bottom of the pass. Slugs sang off rocks and chopped up dirt. The range was no good for accuracy with a submachine gun at this downward angle. But the fury of the barrage had its effect, driving the troopers momentarily back down behind cover. By the time the AR ran out of ammo, Rosen was reloaded and firing again.

Jarrell ripped out the empty magazine and jammed in a loaded one. On the other side of the open stretch, Chalker and Ali reached the rock outcroppings. They turned instantly in its cover, and began firing down into the pass, taking over the job of pinning the troopers down from that angle.

As soon as Venturi's grease gun and Josal's Schmeisser joined in the barrage from the outcroppings, Jarrell nudged Rosen. "Get going."

"What about Gerd?"

"His six minutes are up. *Move.*"

Rosen didn't like it, but he went; sprinting across the open stretch while the barrage from the outcroppings ahead kept the troopers in the bottom of the pass pinned down. Jarrell waited until Rosen's Garand joined in from the outcroppings. The officer and troopers who'd gone up to find Gerd were coming back down toward the pass. Coming fast. They'd have their weapons in range soon.

Jarrell continued to wait. Four more seconds. Gerd came stumbling up onto the ledge, his chest heaving and his breath whistling through clenched teeth. He went past

Jarrell, out across the open space, his legs moving heavily with weariness. Jarrell shoved to his feet and went after him.

No shots came his way. Rosen, Venturi, and Josal were still giving him covering fire as he dodged into the protective outcroppings with them. Beyond them, Chalker had gotten through a pile of boulders with Lepic, Nora, and Ali, heading up a rising ledge that climbed to the top of a sheer cliff. He had an explosive charge ready in one hand.

There were a number of other ways over and around the cliff. But the ledge was the only quick way. Any of the others would cost their pursuers time, leaving them almost half an hour behind.

Jarrell sent Josal and the weary Gerd on ahead through the boulders to the cliff. He looked back over an outcrop into the pass. The officer had all his troops assembled in it now. They were starting up; fanning out to either side in an encircling advance. Each one shifted fast from cover to cover; making for individual, hard-to-hit targets. Coming that way, they had too much fire-power to stave off from a position vulnerable to encirclement. Jarrell glanced toward the cliff. Josal and Gerd were almost to the top. The others were over it, out of sight.

"Come on." Jarrell led Venturi and Rosen through the boulders on the run. They got to the bottom of the rising ledge and began climbing.

A CAL set for full automatic fire began stuttering behind them when they were halfway up. Bullets broke chunks of stone off the cliff in front of Jarrell. Then the barrels of Gerd's rifle and Ali's M-1 poked over the top and fired down. The racket of the CAL stopped.

Several others began stammering from the protection of the boulders below as Jarrell reached the top and swung over. Chalker was crouched down near the edge, setting the charge in a deep crack between two tilting rock formations. Gerd and Ali drew back from the edge and ran crouched to join the others.

A hail of shots from below chewed along the cliff edge as Venturi and Rosen swung over beside Jarrell and started past him. One tugged at Jarrell's left sleeve as he went down flat. Another whispered over him and knocked Rosen forward before he could get down out of sight. He fell across Venturi with a thin cry, a shiny darkness running down his lower back. Venturi seized him and dragged him away from the cliff edge.

Jarrell cursed and twisted, staying flat. The submachine gun jarred in his fists as he slashed a downward burst at the boulders below.

"All set, Captain," Chalker said calmly. "Get gone."

Jarrell eased away from the edge, got his feet under him, and sprinted crouched behind a jutting shoulder of rock. There was a sputtering flash as the fuse ignited. Chalker charged past Jarrell and dove at the ground. The charge went off like a short burst of thunder; a sound that was engulfed by the prolonged noise of falling masses of rock.

And then there was silence. Jarrell stepped out from the rock shoulder and went through a swirling cloud of rising dust to what was left of the cliff top. A huge section of the edge had broken away and fallen. Carefully, he eased forward just enough to squint down.

Most of the rising ledge below was gone. Those troops would have to take the long way up. Jarrell's eyes got a dulled look. He turned from the edge and walked to where the others were gathered.

Venturi sat on the ground, holding Rosen. Jarrell looked, and said nothing. There were no words that would change it: The slug had gone clear through Rosen, widening as it came out the front. His hands were fumbling weakly to stem the gush of blood. But there was no hole to stop up; his whole middle was opened.

Rosen's head sagged limply on Venturi's thick shoulder. "Hell . . ." he whispered. "Oh, hell . . ."

Tears streamed down Venturi's tough, handsome face. "This I swear to you, my friend," he told Rosen thickly. "Your daughter and her mother will be rescued by us. You know from the past what my word means. I swear it."

There was no way of knowing if Rosen had heard any of it. He was dead.

Marcel Venturi continued to hold Rosen and cry. Nora watched him, stunned. She watched, too, the utter lack of any expression in Jarrell's face as he picked up Rosen's rifle and slung it over his own shoulder, then opened Rosen's pack.

He took all the ammunition inside, and passed out the rest from the pack among the others. Next he got everything from Rosen's pockets, including Bishop's power of attorney and the letter of credit. Each had been altered by Simon Bishop's attorney in Palermo, so that either Jarrell or Venturi could execute it, if Rosen wasn't present. Jarrell stuck them in his pocket and stood up.

"Time to go, Marcel."

Venturi looked up at Jarrell, and it seemed to Nora that there was something very dangerous in Venturi's face. "He was my friend."

"He's dead," Jarrell told him harshly, "and you've got to leave him. Right now. The only thing you can do for what's left of him is carry out your vow to him. 'Leave the dead and just keep on going'—the commando survival code, Marcel. And that means getting the hell out of here. *Now.*

Venturi gently lowered Rosen until he lay on the ground. He got to his knees beside the body and folded Rosen's arms on his chest, closed the eyes with his thick thumbs. He continued to kneel beside Rosen for a moment, whispering a short prayer. Then he crossed himself and stood up.

"He was a good man," he told Jarrell tonelessly. "I saved his life twice, in the war."

He walked away from Rosen's body without wiping the tears from his face.

They were up very high now, inside the very heart of the Atlas. The land of the savage tribes from which Bel Zaara had sprung—and Mahjoub Lepic. A desolate country; but one that gave isolation, concealment, and protection.

They went over the lip of a long-dead volcano, across a void of smashed stone. Lepic turned into a tight ravine and led them through to a wide canyon. They followed a steep path clinging to one side of it; a grinding climb that took its toll of their legs and lungs. The path twisted abruptly, down across a bone-dry river bed carpeted with sand, up the high slope on the other side.

Jarrell's gaze roved restlessly from side to side through the trek, studying formations and shadows on either side of their route ahead. Lepic and Ali knew the way; Jarrell left that to them. He was looking for something else.

They climbed to the brow of the hill on the other side, into a cold, stinging wind. Just above them between the peaks, a much stronger wind was tearing clouds into wild shreds. Jarrell brought his force to a halt on the hilltop and looked back, in the direction from which they'd come.

The troops were climbing down from a ridge back there. Jarrell counted sixteen of them. Less than twenty minutes behind.

Jarrell turned again and looked down the other side of the hill. It sloped into a very wide canyon, its harsh, flat bottom strewn with far-spaced boulders and clawed by stony gullies. The boulders were polished and wrinkled from centuries of spring-rain floods. Sparse dry hawthorne grew out of the gullies. On both sides of the wide canyon gaunt masses of rocks piled up against sheer cliffs. The cliffs on one side glowed like heated iron in the fierce rays of the sun. On the other side the cliffs were iron-gray, pocked with black grottos from which water would spout during heavy rains.

In the distance ahead, the cliffs converged until they walled a tight, darkly shadowed pass.

Ali pointed in that direction. "Our way is through there."

Jarrell nodded absently, his slitted eyes surveying all of the wide canyon.

A brief wisp of dust drifted away from a gully. That could be the wind.

Something small was glinting reflected sunlight in the mouth of the distant pass. That could be anything: a flood-polished stone, a piece of broken glass or a discarded tin can left behind by some traveler. Anything.

Then whatever it was stopped glinting.

That meant it had moved.

Jarrell unslung Rosen's Garand and growled, *"On the run."* He sprinted down the slope. The others ran after him. He angled across the canyon floor, toward the iron-gray cliffs. He stopped at the masses of broken rock mounting the base of a cliff in a rising jumble. This presented what they needed now: good defensive cover for a holding action against superior forces.

"Spread out in there," Jarrell told his men in a quick, level voice as they reached him. "Individual cover, spaced well apart to rake all approaches from the flat out here with cross fire."

They moved in past him, fast, Gerd drawing Nora with him to shelter deep inside the rocks. Jarrell stayed where he was, turning his back on the rocks and watching the whole canyon. His finger rested lightly across the trigger of the Garand as his eyes shifted from one point to another, searching. There were no more wisps of dust. No glinting object that moved. No sound.

He was still standing there, in the open, when the first troopers came into sight over the top of the hill. They got a good look at him as he turned and went in among the rocks.

That suited Jarrell.

THIRTEEN

This time they were very cautious. Gerd's shooting in the pass had taught them that much. They didn't make the mistake of a direct attack on the rocks behind which Jarrell's force was barricaded.

Instead, they came down the hill slope, keeping well out of even Gerd's range. And angled away toward the cliffs on the other side of the canyon.

Ali's M-1 snapped a useless shot in their direction.

"Hold your fire!" Jarrell rapped.

He was down on one knee against a high hump of rock, whose shadow hid him as long as he didn't move too much in it. From this position he looked out between two squat boulders that protected him but allowed a full field of vision covering the entire canyon.

The troops were moving along the opposite cliffs, small in the distance as they headed swiftly toward the opening at the other end. Their intention was clear: When they were near the pass they would swing out to good cover, to cut Jarrell's force off from that way out.

Jarrell's lean mouth stretched a little. It might have been a smile.

He counted nine of them. That left seven on the other side of the hill. Undoubtedly well barricaded where they could block any attempt by Jarrell's force to get back over it. They were making the canyon a trap, bottling up both ends.

Earlier, Jarrell's field glasses had showed him one trooper lugging a radio. This one hadn't come over the hill. By now he'd be radioing the position, so a Chinook could fly in with a full load of reinforcements. The helicopter would land the new troops on the cliff above Jarrell's position. They'd have sniper's rifles with them. From up there they'd be able to pick Jarrell's trapped force off at leisure, one by one.

Jarrell waited and watched.

The troops were almost to the pass at the other end of the canyon. Jarrell watched them turn away from the cliff wall, heading out to take up positions in gullies and behind boulders across the mouth of the pass. They moved in a neat, orderly column.

Black cloaked and hooded figures seemed to grow out of the ground on either side of the column before any of the troopers reached cover. The black-shrouded figures rose up only enough to aim the automatic rifles they held. They all began firing at the same time, the sustained hammering of the barrage reverberating through the canyon.

Five troopers went down under that first barrage. The rest broke and ran towards the mouth of the pass; each man going his own way, dodging desperately to get to the next bit of cover.

Fifteen Berber warriors on sturdy mountain ponies rode out of the pass and swept down on them. These warriors, too, were shrouded in fringed hoods and camel-skin *djellebahs* of black, unrelieved except for the dull-red ovals embroidered on their backs. It was said that the red ovals were to make good targets of any Berber who ever turned to run from an enemy. The mounted warriors had automatic weapons, too; but slung across their backs. They slammed into the troopers with long spears and curved swords.

Jarrell stayed where he was, watching it—a short, bloody, one-sided battle out of another century, cavalry against infantry. The infantry, caught in the open and split apart, didn't have a chance, in spite of their rapid-fire assault rifles. The cavalrymen rode them down before they could use their weapons effectively. After that it was close-quarters slaughter; the fast-riding warriors hacking and jabbing with their swords and spears, better than rifles in that tight-packed melee.

It was over quickly; with every trooper dead. The black-shrouded figures who had started the ambush crawled out of their gullies drawing their swords, and began gleefully slashing at the dead bodies. The mounted warriors stayed in their saddles, looking expectantly down the canyon.

Jarrell heard it then, from the other side of the hill—the pounding of many hooves. Bursts of automatic fire began stammering again. And stopped, very quickly. There was a silence—and then twenty mounted, black-clad warriors rode up into view on the brow of the hill.

Seven of them held long spears in upright position. Each spear had a severed head mounted on its point, the fresh blood still dripping.

The mounted warriors from the pass began riding through the canyon. As they came, they exchanged their swords and spears for their automatic rifles. Jarrell leaned the Garand against a rock and unslung the stubby AR, putting it on full automatic. He watched the cavalrymen on the hill ride down, swinging wide of Jarrell's position to join the other force.

The two forces joined, paused, and then began a slow advance toward Jarrell's position. A big, heavy-set rider led them. As they got closer, their faces could be made out inside the black hoods: savage faces, hesitating between blood lust and curiosity.

Jarrell leaned against the jut of rock, holding himself ready. He was counting on their having seen that the army troopers who were their enemy were also the enemy of Jarrell's force. If that didn't mean anything to them, Jarrell's men were barricaded well enough to hold them off. Long enough for the Chinook to arrive. That would pit the warriors against army troops again, giving Jarrell a chance to get his people out in the confusion.

The black-shrouded riders slowed their advance and began spreading out to either side, with their weapons held in firing position. Jarrell's hands tightened around the grips of the AR, one finger sliding across the trigger.

Then Ali rose up from the rocks in plain sight, without the M-1 carbine. His hands were spread open to either side of him, palms toward the mounted warriors. He began speaking very loud and fast in a dialect that Jarrell couldn't follow.

One of the warriors looked at Ali in surprise; then answered in the same tongue. The tone told it: he recognized Ali. The heavy-set Berber leader glanced at him, and snapped a gutteral order. Ali moved down through the rocks toward the warriors, continuing to talk loud and fast all the way. The Berber leader cut him short with a question. Ali answered. More questions and answers. The element of threat began to leave the savage faces.

Ali turned and called to Jarrell: "It is safe. You may come down. I have explained who and what you are. They saw that the army was trying to catch and kill us; so they believe. One of them is from the same village as Yussef, my friend who is in contact with Bel Zaara. He remembered me. This"—Ali indicated the big, heavy-set rider—"is their leader, El Mansour. A great warrior. He is allied with Ben Hafidi, Bel Zaara's uncle."

El Mansour's chin lifted in pride as the name he had chosen for himself was said. A proud name indeed— "the victorious." One of the ninety-nine adjectives for Allah.

"A great warrior," Ali repeated emphatically. "He wishes you to come down."

Jarrell lowered the submachine gun as he stepped into sight from the rocks; but he continued to hold it ready in one hand. He didn't have to tell the others to stay where they were and keep their weapons aimed. El Mansour eyed him with hard interest as he came forward.

Jarrell met the stare with the proper mixture of respect and coolness as he spoke to Ali. "If they're allied to Allal Ben Hafidi, do they know where he is now?"

"I have already asked this. They are not sure, because they have been on raids for some time, out of touch with Ben Hafidi."

"What about the village where your friend Yussef is? Is it safe? Or is the army there?"

Ali translated. El Mansour's answer came with a short, booming laugh.

Ali turned back to Jarrell, grinning appreciatively. "El Mansour says the village is safe. The army was near it—but he wiped out half of it, and chased the rest away."

Jarrell's smile was admiring. "El Mansour earns his name."

El Mansour listened gravely as Ali translated this; then nodded and spoke again.

"He says," Ali told Jarrell, "that he will take us there."

That, Jarrell didn't want—these armed fighting men going with them. They might decide to go along all the way to Bel Zaara, after they reached the village. "Tell El Mansour I appreciate his kind offer. But I think there is something else he would rather do than escort us. Tell him that a big army helicopter is going to show up here soon. It will be carrying about forty soldiers. They will probably land on top of this cliff behind me."

Ali translated this; and Jarrell's explanation of how he knew it. An eager excitement crept into El Mansour's expression. He glanced up the cliff, pondered a moment, and then raised a hand to Jarrell in farewell. Shouting an order, he whirled his horse and led his warriors up over the hill.

Apparently there was a way to the top of the cliff in that direction. The troops landing in that Chinook were going to have a reception committee waiting for them.

Jarrell watched El Mansour's cavalry ride away. "How much further to the village?" he asked Ali.

"This detour the army of the pass forced us to follow has taken us far off the way. We cannot reach it from here until night."

"Then let's get started."

The last Berber warriors disappeared beyond the hill. Jarrell took his force in the opposite direction, through the pass.

Even under the brilliant starlight, the village could hardly be seen. It huddled against the base of a barren mountain slope, merged into its night darkness. If it hadn't been for the smell of wood-and-charcoal fires burning within the village, they could have walked past without noticing it.

Actually, it was composed of two villages. One was a congregation of tattered black tents, set close together around the outside of a low defense wall of piled stones, with two squat, square towers. The other was inside the walls, which curved around it to the wall of the mountain itself. The inner village was a dark cluster of small buildings constructed of packed dirt and rocks. They rose in many levels as they reached the base of the mountain slope. There they climbed it one on top of the other, in steeped-back tiers, the slope itself forming their rear walls, the roof of one building serving as a floor for the one above it.

Jarrell had counted five levels as they waited by the steep path outside. But that wasn't where his attention was now. Shadowy burnoosed figures drifted like ghosts around the outer village, briefly glimpsed, then merged into invisibility against the blackness of the tattered tents. He could feel the pressure of hidden eyes watching from that disordered darkness; speculating, suspicious eyes. There'd be guns in there, too, restrained only by the word Ali had passed as he'd gone in alone.

Nora stepped past Jarrell, studying the night village with interest stronger than the feeling of foreboding emanating from its darkness. Automatically, Jarrell reached out a hand and pulled her back into the shadow of a boulder against which he stood, to make an indistinct target.

Finally, two figures detached from the blackness of the tents, and came toward them. One was Ali. He gestured at the other, taller than he but just as thin in his shabby burnoose.

"This is Yussef."

Nora was looking at Yussef closely. *"You're* the one who took me to Bel Zaara. I remember you—when they took my blindfold off."

Yussef nodded, studying her in turn.

145

Ali said to him, "You see? She *is* the one. Bel Zaara was very pleased we helped her to reach him, that last time. And she vouches for these men." Yussef nodded again; but ingrained suspicion still showed in his face.

Jarrell asked Ali, "You have explained the purpose of our mission to him?"

"Yes. He understands, but——"

"I will speak for myself," Yussef cut in slowly, having trouble with the French words. He peered suspiciously through the dark shadows at them. "I will not lead so many armed men to the place where Bel Zaara hides. That must be understood first."

Nora felt Josal make an involuntary forward movement beside her; was aware of Jarrell's arm stopping him.

"What do you propose, then?" Jarrell asked pleasantly.

"I will take *one* of you. No more. Pick one who can speak with authority of this money matter with Bel Zaara. Only one."

"That's fine with us," Jarrell told him carelessly. "One is all that's necessary for the talking. The rest of us were only to make sure that one got this far." He turned his head to look at Venturi. "That better be you, Marcel."

Nora stared at him.

"Of course," Venturi said. "I am the best one for this sort of thing."

Then Nora understood. Venturi was a natural: a veteran of tense gangland negotiations.

"The rest of you will remain here," Yussef stated flatly. "Until we return. Or Bel Zaara sends for you. Or—"

He didn't continue with the other possibility.

Jarrell nodded. "Agreed."

Yussef smiled, reassured. "Good. Then you will please accept the hospitality of my home now. I cannot go with your man until daylight. The trail is too difficult."

"You'll use horses or mules?" Jarrell asked absently, with no real interest in his voice.

"Impossible, for a climb like that. The only way is on foot."

Ali turned to Jarrell. "I must leave you now. Ben Hafidi

146

has sent an urgent message for El Mansour, through Yussef. Since I know where El Mansour is, I must take it. But I will return. In a day or two."

Jarrell nodded. "We'll be here, waiting."

Yussef watched Ali vanish into the darkness, then led the way in through the village of black tents. Jarrell spoke very softly and quickly to Lepic and Chalker as they followed.

Not a single figure was to be seen among the tents as they passed through. But the pressure of watching eyes was there stronger than before, on either side. They went in through the defense wall by a narrow, covered gateway, and threaded between buildings along dark passages like snaking tunnels through the night. One of the passages took them into a small square with gnarled olive trees around a stone well. They were following Yussef across this square when a scream of agony came up out of the ground beside them.

Nora froze with the others, staring. There was a hole in the ground. The scream, dwindling now to the whimpering moans of a soul in hell, had come from there.

"My God . . .," Nora whispered, her mind numbed by shock. "What *is* that?"

"That is the old well," Yussef said in a mild tone. "Dry now, so we had to drill another. The man in the bottom of it is from another village. He came as a friend, but we learned he was a spy for the government, trying to locate Bel Zaara. He is suffering the punishment of salt as decreed by Bel Zaara."

Having said that much, Yussef moved on uninterestedly. Sick hatred smouldered in Jarrell's eyes as he turned from the torture hole to follow him. His face was a mask of stone.

Another animal howl of pain echoed up out of the disused well. It rooted Nora to the spot, shaking her. Hot nausea rose in her throat. Gerd seized her wrist and dragged her away stumbling after the others.

"What did he mean," she asked thickly, "the punishment of salt?"

147

Gerd drew her with him away from the square. "Never mind."

"An interesting old torture," Josal said, walking on the other side of her. "Devised by the Arabs. The victim's palms are slit wide open with a sharp sword. Raw salt is poured into the bleeding opening and then the tips of his fingers are forced into it. They pull wet oxhide gloves over the closed fists, to make sure he cannot pull his fingers out. Then they tie him securely so he can't remove the shrinking gloves. And leave him. The salt goes on burning the inside of his slashed palms, which his inserted fingertips prevent from healing. His fingernails begin to grow, digging deeper into the open wounds and causing more pain. Pain that never ends, until he dies of tetanus or shock. But that can take two or three weeks."

The screaming rose and fell, following them through the village. It could still be heard as they reached the houses piled up against the base of the mountain slope. Gerd had to help Nora up a ladder to the roof of one building. Her legs wouldn't work properly. Her mind wouldn't leave the square.

They climbed another ladder, onto a second roof, with the mass of dark rock hanging above them. Yussef pulled aside a curtain and ushered them in. Jarrell had to lower his head to get under the low doorway. The small room inside was bare of furniture. Only worn Berber rugs and woven mats on the clay floor, grouped around a small charcoal fire that heated and lit the room.

While his guests settled on the rugs and mats, Yussef went through another curtained doorway. He returned with a pot of tea and small cups on a brass tray. In silence, they drank the traditional three cups of the mint-flavored tea. Except Nora, who leaned against the wall hugging herself with her arms, listening to the still dimly heard screams.

Mahjoub Lepic finished his third cup of tea and looked at Jarrell. "I think that I have completed the job I agreed to do for you. I have escorted you this far. You are here, with no further need for me. And I have other business to attend to back in Marrakesh. If you agree, I will start back immediately."

Jarrell took the time required for thinking it over. "All right. As you say, there's no further need for your services."

"Then if you will pay me now, so I can leave?"

Jarrell got Rosen's checkbook out, and a pen.

As he made out the check, Chalker said: "Since Lepic knows the way, I'd like to go back with him, Jarrell." He spoke in French, for Yussef to understand. "I got some friends waiting for me at home. And you don't need me to help you just sit here and wait."

Jarrell shrugged. "I have no objections. The job you agreed on is finished." He gave the check to Lepic, and made out another for Chalker.

Sticking it in his pocket, Chalker stood up with Lepic. "Well, see you around sometime, Jarrell. Nice doing business with you."

He waved farewell and followed Lepic out. Jarrell held his empty cup to Yussef, who refilled it.

As he sipped at the hot brew, Jarrell glanced toward Nora huddled against the wall. "I am afraid," he told Yussef gently, "that she is disturbed by the cries of your village prisoner."

"Ah?" Yussef looked curiously at Nora. "Interesting. *Our* women find it amusing."

"The ways of women *are* interesting," Jarrell said blandly. "I think it would be best for the sleep of this one, if we make our camp tonight outside your village. Where she cannot hear his screams."

"In the open?"

"We are used to that."

Yussef shrugged, and eyed Nora speculatively again. "If that is your wish."

"You are kind." Jarrell took his time finishing the last cup of tea before standing.

"I will find you at dawn," Yussef told him. "I will take this man." He nodded at Venturi. "The rest of you will remain behind."

Jarrell nodded. "As agreed."

149

"You will remain behind in the open; where I can see you from a long way off. If you attempt to follow us, I will go no further."

Jarrell looked into Yussef's eyes. "We will not follow you." He helped Nora to her feet and took her out with him. Venturi, Josal, and Gerd nodded to Yussef and went out after them.

They had to go through the village square again to reach the gate in the walls. Jarrell put his arm around Nora tightly, hurrying her through. He could feel her whole body shuddering against him; could feel, too, the sickening shocks hitting all of his own nervous system.

It was one thing to have to absorb something like that yourself. Letting yourself feel what it was doing to some-one else made it that much harder. Which was why he learned long ago not to let himself feel through anyone else. But now, it was happening again. And he couldn't stop it happening.

They settled down to sleep on a flat-topped rise out-side the village. It was a long time, in spite of her weari-ness, before Nora could sleep. She lay rolled tightly on her side on the ground, aware of Jarrell whispering with Ven-turi nearby. But it was what she could not hear—except inside her head—that kept her from sleep.

The animal screams of agony from the bottom of that hole inside the village.

Never ending.

FOURTEEN

Jarrell squinted against the harsh morning light, watching Yussef and Venturi climb to a slope of bare, splintered rock. By the time they reach its crest to the south, they'd be half a mile away. And beyond that undoubtedly lay a maze in which someone of Yussef's experience could vanish with Venturi; over stony ground where they'd leave no tracks anyone could follow.

Jarrell remained standing on a hilltop with Gerd and Josal as instructed; where Yussef could see them each time he glanced back. Nora sat on a hump of rock near them, also watching. Her face was haggard; her eyes dulled, listless. She hadn't said a word since waking that dawn.

Jarrell moved over to her without taking his eyes off the figures of Yussef and Venturi, getting smaller up the slope. "I'm sorry we had to bring you," he said quietly. "But it *was* necessary. Yussef might not have believed me, if you weren't along. Even so, I wish you weren't here. And that you didn't have to go on with us. But we can't leave you behind alone."

She heard the undercurrent of feeling behind the words; but her own feelings were still too choked down to respond. "You didn't bring me. I came. My choice. Don't worry about me, I'll be all right. I was shook up by . . . that man's screaming. I'm still shook up. I've heard men suffering before, on the battlefield, in field hospitals. But something like this . . . so deliberately inflicted. So fiendish . . ." She shook her head in an attempt to banish the memory. "I'll get over it eventually, I imagine."

"No," Jarrell said softly. "Some things nobody ever quite gets over."

Nora studied him, surprised; and then not surprised. "It shook you, too."

"I'm human." He said it without rancor or humor.

"Yes . . ." She looked from his profile to what he was watching: Venturi and Yussef getting smaller in the distance. "Where are Lepic and Chalker?"

Jarrell nodded slightly toward a tall pinnacle rising above the crest of the slope to the southeast, and another to the southwest. "There, and there. Wherever Bel Zaara has those women, it can't be back in the direction we've come from. So Yussef had to head in that general direction; up between them, or to either side."

"You're sure they can keep track of Yussef and your friend, without being spotted?"

"They'll have to." There was a strain in his voice that Nora hadn't heard before.

She studied him for a moment. "What's Venturi suppose to do—knock Yussef out as soon as he knows where Bel Zaara is, and wait for us to catch up?"

"No. He's got to go in, and put the proposition to Bel Zaara."

"Then you figure there *is* a chance Bel Zaara will accept it."

"No chance at all. Bel Zaara won't release those women. Not for money."

Nora frowned at him uncertainly. "And knowing that, Venturi is still going in to try it."

"There's no other way to find out where their sentries are," Jarrell said simply. "And no other way to find out exactly where they've got the hostages."

He glanced at her. His eyes were iron-stubborn. "I'm going to get those women *out*."

"I know that," she told him quietly. "If anyone can. I think Venturi was right about you."

"It's not just for the money." The words reached for understanding; but not the tone.

"I know that, too." Nora hesitated. "But it must be very hard for you—to send a friend into something like that, alone. Even though I know an officer has to be able to handle that kind of responsibility. For other peoples' lives."

Jarrell looked away. "I used to be able to handle it." He was silent for a long moment. "I'm getting too old."

The strain showed on his face, too, now. Nora didn't say anything.

Without looking at her again, he said: "Josal has Rosen's revolver. I think you should take it now. Just in case. Have Josal show you how to use it."

She thought about the man in the torture hole, suffering the punishment of salt. "All right." She got to her feet. "But only to use on myself, if it comes to that."

"That's what I meant."

She went behind him to Josal and Gerd. Jarrell kept watching the slope.

Yussef and Venturi had reached the top of it.

Yussef paused with Venturi on the crest and turned to look back down the slope. His sharp eyes made out each figure distinctly: Jarrell, Gerd, Josal, and the woman. All still where he'd left them; where they were supposed to be. Yussef relaxed, and led Venturi down the slope on the other side. Even if those people back there tried to follow now, by the time they could reach that crest, Yussef and Venturi would have vanished. With no way for anyone to guess which direction they'd taken.

Yussef angled to the southwest, entering a labyrinth of towering rocks. Within minutes they were deep within the maze, with the crest blocked from sight behind them. Every dozen steps there was another choice of directions. The ground was hard, taking no impression of their passing. Yussef kept Venturi beside him, so he could drop nothing to reveal their route.

"How far is it?" Venturi asked him.

"We should get there by one hour past noon, if we

153

move quickly." Yussef stopped and looked at Venturi. "From here on, you must be blindfolded. I am sorry, but it is required."

Venturi shrugged. "Okay." He was thinking about what Jarrell had told him—to try to delay getting to Bel Zaara until as close to night as possible.

Yussef tied a black cloth across his eyes, blocking out light and vision. "I will hold your wrist and lead you. Do not be afraid. Just lift your feet well as we go."

"Not too fast," Venturi grumbled. "I'm not as young as I used to be."

Yussef tugged him along. Venturi stumbled; and took time regaining his balance.

A small point of reflected light winked from the top of the high pinnacle to the southwest.

That was Mahjoub Lepic.

Jarrell got a small steel mirror from his pocket and held it so it caught the sunlight, sending back answering blinks of acknowledgment. Then he turned the mirror until it reflected toward the pinnacle to the southeast, flashing code signals. After a moment there were acknowledgment blinks from Chalker.

Jarrell put away the mirror and slung his pack on his back. He led Gerd, Nora, and Josal down off the hill and up the long bare slope. Not up the middle, as Yussef and Venturi had gone; angling up to the southwest side of it. Climbing with long, driving strides that ate up space swiftly.

When he was up under the top of the slope, Jarrell paused. Then he eased up just a bit more; raising his head over the crest only enough to see down into the labyrinth of rocks spreading away below the other side. He scanned from side to side, searching. Lepic would be tailing by now, with the mirror hung on the back of his head where it was bound to reflect light from time to time. But in that maze of high, twisted rock, nothing showed but still shadows. Jarrell waited.

Chalker came puffing up the slope behind them, and flopped down to catch his breath. Still no blinking came to signal the way. They went on waiting, with the tension coiling tighter.

Then it came: small flashes of reflected sunlight, moving up over another ridge on the other side of the labyrinth. Still angling southwest.

Jarrell swung over the crest and led the way down through the maze of rocks.

An hour later they caught up with Mahjoub Lepic. He was crouched under the shade of a shale overhang, high on a mountainside, squinting across a series of ridges to the south. As the others came in beside him, he silently removed the mirror from the back of his head and pointed.

It took Jarrell a moment to locate the two small figures, moving around a bulging slope in the distance.

"They are slow," Josal observed.

"Venturi's having some trouble," Jarrell told him dryly. "Old legs."

He gave his field glasses to Chalker. "I'll trail now. The rest of you stay well behind. Just keep me in sight."

He went out beyond the overhang immediately, making a number of detours to keep to cover all the way as he headed for the distant slope; moving fast to make up the time the detours cost him.

Venturi and Yussef were no longer visible to the others, and Jarrell's distant figure just barely in sight, when Chalker took them after him beyond the overhang.

"The idea being," Josal explained to Nora, "that if we traveled in a bunch, as close to Yussef as Jarrell is, there would be too much chance of being spotted."

"I understood that," Nora told him. "And I suppose there's no chance of Yussef looking back and spotting Jarrell."

Chalker laughed.

Gerd said politely, "I assure you, no one Jarrell stalks ever knows he is there. Until it is too late for them."

Marcel Venturi stumbled blindly and fell, rolling against a boulder. He groaned and held his knee with both hands, lying on his side.

155

Yussef hastily squatted beside him, worried. "Are you hurt?"

"My goddam leg," Venturi snarled. "I think I sprained it. It's this lousy blindfold."

"I am sorry," Yussef told him firmly, "but it is necessary. Can you stand?"

"Help me up, and let's find out."

Yussef helped him to his feet. Venturi spread his legs, balancing and testing. He winced. "It hurts like hell. But I can walk. If you take it easy."

Yussef took hold of his hand, and led him on. Venturi leaned against him, limping with every other step.

It slowed them down considerably.

Jarrell slowed to the same pace only when he was very close to them. Too close, except for a man with experience at this kind of stalking. There were periods when he was actually moving parallel to them, others when he dropped behind. It depended on the terrain. At times he had them in sight; but more often he trailed them by the dust they raised, or by picking a route they must take because there was no alternative.

All of him felt electrically alive, sharply tuned to every nuance of what he was doing. It was at moments like this that he knew this was the work he'd been born to; savoring the taste of functioning well at it for the last time. One part of him took care of moving him always in cover at the best distance, automatically placing his steps so they raised a minimum of dust and started no loose stones rolling. The rest of him kept track of the pair he was trailing, and studied places where watchers might be lurking in the changing terrain.

They were over the rocky spine of the mountain range now, beginning to work downward along the other side. The heat was increasing drastically; a dry, baking heat sweeping up between the southern slopes from the Sahara. The highest cliffs and ridges still hung far above them. But now there were glimpses between broken walls and contorted formations of what lay below: a descending desolation of white limestone and gray granite and black lava rock, of blinding sunlight and impenetrable shadows; a flash of green bordering a stream that sprang out of one cave and battered its way down through tight winding gorges before vanishing into another; limp, brown palms marking a small oasis on the lower slopes.

And below and beyond all the desert, an undulating sea of burning sand and rocks spreading southward endlessly under the glare of a sky like an inverted bowl of heated gold; vast, empty, lonely, and dead.

Jarrell tailed Yussef and Venturi down over dried-out clay webbed with wide cracks, through rocks and gullies the color of saffron. He knew it had to be close now; very close.

It was late afternoon when Yussef led the blindfolded, limping Venturi into a deep, narrow canyon. They stopped just inside the entrance. Yussef let go of Venturi's hand and raised both arms high, looking up and loudly calling a password.

A lean, black-robed figure emerged from a shadowed formation on the left wall above them, aiming a rifle down. He called a sharp question. Yussef answered loudly, identifying himself and explaining the presence of the stranger with him. The dark figure of a second sentry stepped out of a black grotto high in the right wall. He turned away, cupping both hands around his mouth and calling out shrilly. The cry echoed away down the corridor of the canyon, carrying far. Yussef stayed where he was with Venturi, waiting.

Jarrell angled away from the canyon entrance, climbing up to the right of it between mammoth blocks of red-veined granite and mounds of shattered shale. He climbed swiftly, but careful to make little sound and stir up no dust. When he was above and behind the position of the sentry on the right wall, he went to ground. Raising himself just a bit on elbows and toes, he snaked forward until he could peer over the top.

From this point he couldn't see Venturi and Yussef in the canyon entrance below, or either of the sentries. What he could see was a straight length of canyon cutting south for about seven hundred yards before it made a sharp bend. Horsemen came riding around the bend and thundered through the corridor toward the canyon entrance. They were warriors of various nations—Arabs, Tauregs, and Chleuhs. Their weapons were equally varied—rifles, spears, swords, submachine guns. They vanished below Jarrell, into the canyon entrance.

He used the wait that followed to survey the immediately surrounding area. This canyon was the way in, no question about that. There was no other way that could be used by horse or mule. A man afoot was another matter; for this there were a number of different possibilities. Jarrell studied them, deciding on the best.

Chalker crept in behind Jarrell and stretched out beside him. He made no sound; just watched.

The mounted warriors came riding back into the straight stretch of canyon below. They rode their horses at a slow walk, in two columns of five riders each. Yussef and Venturi walked between them. Venturi's blindfold had been removed; also his weapons.

Jarrell eased back away from the edge. Chalker did the same. Jarrell took the field glasses from him, pointed, and set off in a low crouch, following shadows and rock cover as he followed a circuitous route toward the inner bend of the canyon.

Chalker waited until the others reached him. Then he led them after Jarrell, keeping them down low and following exactly the route Jarrell had used.

Jarrell passed the bend of the canyon, circled away from it, then angled back toward where it led. From time to time he paused to scan his altered surroundings, and reexamine each shadowed place from the changed angle. Each time, he did not move on until he'd made sure there was no one to observe his going. When he did shift position, he moved swiftly with a smooth ease that made it seem lazy.

He reached a break in the rocks, eased through, and came to a stop. There was a short open space ahead of him, and then a drop. There was also a sentry on a ledge four hundred yards away.

The sentry wasn't looking in Jarrell's direction at the moment. But he would, eventually. The shadows in the break would conceal Jarrell, as long as he held still. But he had to get out on that open space, for a better look at what lay below the drop. Quickly, Jarrell lowered his pack to the ground, then his weapons, which would encumber him and might betray him by reflecting light. Then he waited, watching the sentry.

Chalker had halted the others in cover behind Jarrell. They hunched down, watching Jarrell wait, not knowing what he was waiting for. Nora got the same odd feeling she'd had once before, of watching a man on the verge of explosive action though he was absolutely motionless. A coiled spring of a man; strangely dangerous. Strange, too, the sense of protection she felt now, only looking at him there.

The sentry turned in his direction, his hooded eyes searching. They scanned slowly past Jarrell's shadow, and did not return to it. The sentry turned to look in another direction. Jarrell waited until the sentry turned further away, and went quickly through the break, out of its shadow into the open.

He went down flat at the edge of the drop, and became motionless as the ground on which he lay. The sentry would look in his direction again; and now Jarrell was out in the open where he could be seen. But he'd learned long ago that at a distance, what did not move merged into the general landscape. The sentry's eyes would travel past him without communicating what they saw to his brain. Because they wouldn't expect him to be there. They'd be searching the obvious hiding places; not dwelling on places with no concealment to see if there was something just a bit strange about them.

Jarrell was careful not to let any part of him move again; except his eyes, taking in what lay below the drop. The canyon opened there into a wide stony expanse, encircled by what had once been the rim of a volcano. Thousands of years had filled in the volcano's mouth, and eroded the rim down to a series of broken ridges. Enclosed within the remains of that rim was a vast, fire-blackened complex of ruins; interlocked fortress-villages of mud and rock, destroyed, rebuilt, expanded, and destroyed again over the centuries.

A monument to the proud ambition of many conquerors, and the destructive vengeance of many others. Jarrell knew there could only be one mountain stronghold this great in size. Once it had been known as the castle of three hundred rooms and one thousand doors; a maze in which a man might wander for hours without finding his way from the kitchens to the harem, even if he carried the huge number of keys, each of which opened only one of the doors.

The last lord of the mountains to reign here was long dead. So was the chieftain who'd swept up from the desert to vanquish him and devastate this symbol of his power. What remained was still grimly formidable. But the thick defense walls had gaping holes and the huge black guard towers were half collapsed. The interior buildings were disintegrating back to shapeless mounds of mud and stones; and most of the roofs had fallen in, scattering their green tiles in heaps across once bright courtyards now buried in sand and dust.

All this was old. What was new were the groups of black tents scattered among the broken walls and collapsing buildings, where a plane flying over would not be able to distinguish them from the fire-blackened ruins and surrounding lava rocks. And the place was crawling with well-armed warriors. Jarrell estimated over a hundred of them. With a pair standing guard at each way in.

Jarrell considered the one thing he could not see, which would still be left from the past: the dungeons under the ruins. If Michele Bishop and Diana Rosen were being kept here, they would be in one of those. But in which one, under which of the interlocking fortress ruins, and to be reached through which crumbling doorway, he could not know. Marcel Venturi's movements would have to show him that.

Jarrell's eyes slid to the end of the canyon. The ten riders were walking their stocky mountain barbs out of it, with Venturi and Yussef between them. Jarrell watched them enter the ruins.

Venturi was brought to a stop in front of a large square building whose roof was gone but whose thick walls remained. There were even still traces of whitewash around the doorway and loophole windows. The ten warriors who had brought him through the canyon formed a semicircle behind him. Yussef was taken inside. Other warriors crowded around, eyeing him with cold curiosity. Venturi's own expression was cold and remote, as though unaware of them. He gazed at the building and waited, standing in the hot late-afternoon sunlight.

Yussef did not come out again. Instead, two big slaves with swords hanging from red-and-blue cords emerged carrying a gilt and brocade chair. They set it down in the shade. Venturi moved to sit in it. A hand reached out and stopped him, and the eyes watching grew colder.

The slaves drew their swords and took positions on each side of the chair. A grossly fat man with flowing white robes and a diseased face came out of the building, followed by a stocky man in an army officer's uniform and a lean young man with the face of a cruelly intelligent hawk. These two took positions to either side. The fat one lowered himself into the chair, and eyed Venturi.

"I am Allal Ben Hafidi," he said softly. "Tell me why you have come here."

"I want a chair," Venturi told him coolly.

Colonel Omrani made a growling sound. "You were asked a question. Answer it."

Venturi ignored him, keeping his eyes on Ben Hafidi. "I have come here to discuss a matter of business with you. When men of honor conduct business negotiations, they sit facing each other, so they may read each other's faces. A chair, please."

Allal Ben Hafidi actually smiled. He snapped out an order. A warrior dashed into the building. He came out with a wooden stool, which he put down in front of Ben Hafidi.

Venturi sat on it, and nodded. "Thank you," he said

in a businesslike voice. "Now— My name is Marcel Venturi. I represent Simon Bishop, who is naturally very concerned about the safety of his wife and daughter."

Bel Zaara looked angrily at his uncle. "You see? My agents were right. The government has no intention of fulfilling our demands. Bishop knows this, so he sends a man to plead with us."

Venturi frowned at him, showing annoyance at the interruption. Ben Hafidi said, "This is my nephew. Bel Zaara. Perhaps it is to *him* you should be speaking."

Venturi shook his head. "I speak to the man in control. And his information is out of date. It's true the government was ready to refuse your demands. But Mr. Bishop has since been applying a great deal of personal pressure —through bribes to the king's advisors, and an offer of creating new industry in this country. I believe, as Mr. Bishop does, that they will yield to this pressure, and release the prisoners you listed."

Bel Zaara regarded him without belief. "Then why has Bishop sent you?"

Venturi kept his eyes on Allal Ben Hafidi. "As I was saying, Mr. Bishop is most concerned for the safety of his wife and daughter—"

Ben Hafidi nodded sympathetically. "This is most understandable. I have family of my own; children I cherish deeply. I would feel as he must, were our positions reversed."

"That is why he sent me to you," Venturi resumed blandly. "I have an offer, to insure their safety. But first, I must see them; to be certain they are at least alive, before I make this offer."

"The Bishop females are alive," Ben Hafidi assured him. "And unharmed in any way. You have my word for this, so you have no need to see them."

Venturi looked confused. "You mean they're not here, where you can show them to me?"

"They *are* here," Ben Hafidi told him flatly. "My meaning was that my word should suffice."

Venturi sighed, and raised a hand to scratch his ear. It

didn't mean anything to anyone—except one man watching from above.

"Very well," Venturi said, and drew the letter of credit from his pocket. "This is Simon Bishop's offer." He gave it to Ben Hafidi. "You will see it is for one million dollars. Payable to Bel Zaara or anyone he designates. When your two hostages arrive safely out of this country. You'll notice that part cannot be revoked. The payment is definite."

Ben Hafidi passed the paper on to Bel Zaara, who glanced through it, and shook his head. "The answer is No. This amount of money means nothing. We have been promised much more than this—"

Ben Hafidi made a scornful sound. "From Syria and Libya? I have seen many promises, but no money."

"We need a success first," Colonel Omrani reminded him. "*Then* the money will come."

"Perhaps." There was a world of cynicism in Allal Ben Hafidi's voice. "I do not believe in what I do not see." He looked again at Venturi. "But one thing I do believe in: We have given our word that the two Bishop women will be killed if the government does not give in to our demands. Mr. Bishop's offer is generous, but cannot change that."

Venturi was silent for a second, absorbing the certainty that there was no way to change their minds. "I'm afraid you misunderstood me," he said smoothly. "This offer is not intended as a substitute for the government here giving in to you. As I said, we believe the government *will* give in. This offer is in addition to that—a good-will gesture, to insure the safety of Mr. Bishop's family. The government will grant your demands, *and* you also get the one million dollars from Mr. Bishop, when his women are safely out of the country."

"I don't believe any of it," Bel Zaara stated flatly.

Allal Ben Hafidi was thoughtful, studying Venturi, who returned his stare with bland sincerity.

"We have nothing to lose," Ben Hafidi decided finally. "I have already decreed that we would wait. It is only two days more. *You* may wait with us; in the company

163

of the two hostages whose welfare so concerns you. If it turns out that you are lying, or wrong, you will die the same death as they."

"I don't lie," Venturi told him with grave dignity, "and I am not wrong. I'm contented to wait." He got to his feet. "Now I'd like to have some sleep. I'm very tired from all the walking."

Ben Hafidi nodded, and told two of his men to take Venturi to the same cell as the women. They gripped his arms on either side, leading him away through the ruins, to what remained of the middle fortress.

There they took him into what had once been the garrison building for the fortress army. Its roof was gone, but the lower walls were intact. Venturi saw a hole in the ground, and stone steps leading down into darkness.

He held back for a moment, looking down into it. Praying that Jarrell was someplace with a clear view of where he was being taken now.

The two warriors pulled him down the steps, into the hole. There were dim corridors, and other stone stairways going even lower, and then a final low passageway, enclosed in solid stone. An oil lamp on a wall hook revealed a guard with a submachine gun sitting on the stone floor outside a heavy, locked door. Venturi's escorts told him Ben Hafidi's orders.

He got up and drew the locking bolts, swinging the door open. Michele and Diana crouched on the floor inside, arms coming up to shield their eyes from the sudden, painful light. A hand flattened against Venturi's back and pushed him into the small cell. The door was pulled shut and locked behind him.

Venturi leaned his back against it and said softly into the total darkness: "Ladies, allow me to introduce myself. My name is Marcel Venturi. Diana, I am here for your father—your former husband, Mrs. Bishop. . . ."

FIFTEEN

The timing involved in changes of the guard is dictated by practicality, and therefore is predictably the same for all armies. Including guerrilla armies. Shortly after dark two mounted warriors, having had their evening meal, rode from the ruins and through the canyon to relieve the sentries out in the entrance.

They reined to a stop in the night-shadowed canyon mouth, and dismounted. The pair who had been on duty through the late afternoon and evening climbed down from their perches, mounted the stocky horses, and rode off through the canyon toward their stronghold in the ruins. The two who remained strolled toward the opposite walls, to climb up and begin their night shift on sentry duty.

The one who approached the left wall was about to begin his climb when Mahjoub Lepic came up on one knee from the dark cliff-base in front of him and wrenched the loosely held rifle out of his left hand. Simultaneously, before the man could cry out, Jarrell's left arm snapped tight across his throat from behind and strangled it. Jarrell's left knee came up into the small of the sentry's back and arched him forward against the strangling arm. The point of the sharp, double-edged knife in Jarrell's right fist explored the sentry's back, found the space between two ribs, and sank in deep.

Jarrell maintained his pressure on the embedded knife

and sliced it to the right, away from the spine. Lepic came to his feet wrapping both arms around the wriggling sentry, holding him in place until his body became a limp dead weight. Then they lowered the body soundlessly to the ground.

Turning quickly, Jarrell looked across the canyon mouth. The figures of Chalker and Gerd rose from the other sentry, killed with equal silence. Jarrell looked down the canyon. The two relieved sentries were still in sight, riding away. They had heard nothing.

Jarrell didn't make another move until the two riders vanished around the inside bend. Then he crouched, wiped his knife clean in the dirt, and removed the dead man's burnoose. Jarrell got into it, pulling the hood over his head to shadow his face. Now he looked no different from many of the warriors in Ben Hafidi's camp. Unless someone saw his face too closely; or noticed the bloody rip in the garment's back.

Jarrell knew that he would have to keep away from lighted places as much as possible. His boots would not give him away. Many of the guerrillas were wearing boots taken from slaughtered troopers. Across the canyon mouth, Chalker was getting into the burnoose of the other dead sentry. With Gerd wearing Nora's, and Lepic in his own, there was nothing about them to draw special attention—if they could get inside the enemy camp without their arrival being noticed.

Jarrell picked up the stubby AR submachine gun and hung it over his shoulder. He had left the Garand behind, with Gerd's Lee-Enfield. They were taking in with them only weapons intended for close-quarters fighting. Lepic had the repeating shotgun and Chalker the M-16, set for automatic fire. Gerd had traded his shotgun to Josal for the Schmeisser machine pistol.

None of them had his pack any longer. They were stripped for action. Under the burnoose, each had his handgun and knife. Plus extra ammo and grenades, hung from a cord around the waist.

The pack with the radio was hidden with Nora just outside the canyon mouth. Jarrell had showed her how to use it, and explained with the map the escape route she must follow on her own, in case none of them made it back out to her. He'd marked out the signal she must send when she got to a certain point at the southern base of the mountains. The radio was already set to the right frequency to bring a Bishop helicopter to her from across the southern border in Spanish Sahara.

He'd made it quite plain that he fully expected they'd make it back out to her with the hostages. He hadn't said that if they didn't, her chances of actually finding her way to the escape point on her own were very dim indeed.

Santiso Josal came into the canyon mouth lugging a full pack on each shoulder. "Still all clear," he whispered. "No one coming yet."

That was the danger they couldn't do anything against: that some warriors might ride in before they reached their objective, and raise an alarm when they found no sentries in the canyon mouth. The only way to cut down the chance of that was to get in and out fast. Jarrell and Lepic started through the canyon along the darkness of one wall, Chalker and Gerd along the other.

Josal followed them part way, and then dropped behind for the preparations that would become necessary if they had to come back out fast under emergency conditions. Jarrell had chosen him for the stay-behind job because his left arm was still too stiff to be used without awkwardness.

It took two hands to do knife work swiftly and silently. And Jarrell's orders allowed no exceptions: On the way in, until they had reached the two women hostages, no one was to use anything *but* a knife, for any reason. And not after they had the women, either, if gunplay could still be avoided.

It was just possible that they could get Venturi and the two women, and then get out again before Ben Hafidl's whole army was aroused.

Possible—but not likely. Therefore Josal's preparations for a desperately hasty retreat.

They turned the bend in the canyon without running into anyone riding out; followed it until they were almost to the end where the canyon opened out. They paused there, Jarrell and Lepic pressed against the darkness of one wall, Chalker and Gerd hidden in the shadow of the opposite wall. Then both pairs eased forward. They could now see the small fires of Ben Hafidi's warriors ahead of them, among the ruins rising starkly under the starlight. They could also see two armed guards right in front of them, stationed outside a gaping opening that had once been the main gate through the outer defense wall.

There was no way to slip around them to any of the other holes in the wall without being spotted. They were blocking the way in, and certain to question everyone who tried to pass, no matter how they were dressed.

There was no need for a consultation now. Jarrell had sketched a detailed layout of the place for his men, showing them exactly where they had to get to, and methodically rehearsing procedures for every possible emergency they might encounter. Jarrell and Lepic stepped away from the base of their wall. They strolled out of the end of the canyon toward the two armed guards.

The guards turned slightly to face them, with their weapons in their hands. One of them snapped a soft challenge, in a dialect Jarrell didn't understand. But it was only a routine gesture at that point. The guards saw nothing in the manner or dress of the approaching pair to alarm them. They didn't even raise their weapons, still held in only one hand, all the way up to firing position.

Lepic began to give an unhurried, sleepy answer, in his own Berber dialect. He and Jarrell continued to close in on the guards at a lazy stroll as he rambled on about what they were doing there. He was still explaining, and they were very close, when Chalker and Gerd came out of the shadows behind the guards.

Each landed on the back of a guard, one hand snapping around across the mouth and the other driving in a knife. In the same instant Jarrell and Lepic leaped forward, each whipping a knife from his robes and slashing deep across the wrist of one guard's weapon-holding hand.

They caught the weapons as they fell from the nerve-severed hands, put them down quietly, and helped Gerd and Chalker hold the guards through their dying. When it was over, they were lowered to the ground. Jarrell glanced around quickly to see if anyone had wandered between them and the broken walls that hid them from the camp inside. There was no one in sight. The killing of the guards had been unobserved. But it wouldn't remain unknown for long. Soon, someone was bound to come by there. Then the whole army inside the ruins would come dangerously alive, very fast.

They drew their knives out of sight within their robes and strolled in through the gap in the walls, making no effort at concealment, as though they'd satisfied the challenge of the guards outside and been passed through. Some cactus grew out of the packed earth of the once solid wall ends on either side of them. The caved-in towers that had guarded the gateway were now crowded with the big, messy nests of storks. Ten yards inside the gateway a large group of armed men sat around a fire in front of a cluster of low, black tents.

Jarrell angled away from the fire, holding himself erect as he led Lepic, Gerd, and Chalker around the side of the tent cluster. A burnoosed warrior with a pair of cartridge belts across his chest and a curved knife hanging from a waist cord came around the other way and walked into Jarrell. He stumbled back, cursing viciously, reaching for his knife.

Jarrell lowered his head to keep his face shadowed by the hood. Lepic stepped past him, hurriedly offering an apology.

"A thousand pardons for this accident. My friend is weary from his long ride. Weary—and in haste, for he bears a personal message for Allal Ben Hafidi."

The warrior thought about Ben Hafidi and dropped his hand from his knife. Grumbling, he brushed past them to join his companions around the fire. Jarrell drew a slow breath and moved on past the tents, picking a route through the ruins that was circuitous and time consuming, but kept them away from tents and fires.

They went through deep shadow between roofless walls that had once enclosed a palace reception hall, turned

169

into a dark alley that had been a paneled, carpeted corridor into the heart of the palace complex. Segments of the carpet remained, spongy with rot under their boots; the wall panels were flaking charcoal. They passed doorways leading into darkness on either side of them, some with heavy doors still hanging open inside them. The corridor ruins made a sharp turn, and suddenly there was bright lamplight in a room ahead; and voices, many voices, raised in argument.

Jarrell got his team back around the corner and turned into one of the dark doorways. Tiles cracked under their feet as they felt their way across the room inside towards a point where the blackness gave way to light. It became a doorway, leading into a large room whose ceiling lay shattered on the floor. There were several big windows, but these were barred by wrought-iron latticework. Jarrell led the other three through a doorway on the other side of the room.

It took them into a similar roofless room. The floor a mess of smashed tiles, burned ceiling timbers, and big velvet cushions thick with mold, close-spaced iron grilles in the windows. Shreds of satin curtains dangling on walls still retaining patches of bright mosaic decoration. Two more doorways with delicately carved Saracenic arches.

They were inside the harem. Jarrell took the left doorway, into the remains of a ruined room. This one had a whole wall missing. It had joined the rest of the rubble and dust spread outside across a big circular courtyard, where once fountains had flowed and flowers had bloomed and caged birds had sung—while somewhere beneath people shrieked and groaned in dank, windowless dungeons.

The dungeons were still there; and they were still too far from the one into which Jarrell had seen Venturi taken. He stood still for a long moment, listening. There were no sounds of other men out there. They crossed the courtyard ruins spread apart, each man with a knife in hand, watching the dark windows and doorways all around them.

Jarrell turned into a narrow corridor of semidarkness,

slippery with sand and littered with pieces of fallen beams. Then they were out in the open again, under the starlight, between cracked and tottering buildings. A street littered with clay-brick rubble led to a disintegrating courtyard. This one was cramped between sagging ruins of interlocking buildings and a high defense wall overgrown with brownish moss.

A curved tunnel had been cut through the wall, which was unusually thick at this point. It was the joining of two walls, where separate fortresses had spread to meet each other. The one on the other side held Michele Bishop, Diana Rosen, and Marcel Venturi.

Jarrell went in first. He went quietly, keeping to one side of the tunnel. His sense of hearing, keyed to the slightest sound, detected a faint murmur of voices beyond the other end of the tunnel. He paused just before the tunnel end. His fingers flexed around the hilt of the commando knife, securing their grip, holding it low with the sharp blade pointing up and out ready for the thrust. Then he eased forward with his narrowed eyes swiftly searching the dark shadows on the other side.

A wide passageway led straight ahead, with a break in the building walls on its left. At the other end of the passage, much too close, four figures squatted around a cooking fire on a mound of rubble from a demolished house. Jarrell recognized the smells of mint-flavored tea and boiled mutton.

He drew the knife out of sight inside the folds of his burnoose, but continued to hold it securely as his free hand reached back and gestured. Lepic came soundlessly beside him; Chalker and Gerd behind. Giving them a moment to see the danger, Jarrell strolled out of the tunnel. Lepic walked beside him, mumbling as though having a conversation with Jarrell. Chalker and Gerd followed them through the passageway in the direction of the men around the fire.

There was no way to avoid being seen by them; but also no reason for the men at the fire to become suspicious. The thing was not to get too close.

One of the men at the fire raised a beckoning hand.

"Comrades," he called, "come and join our circle. There is food enough for all."

To Jarrell's ears, the tone of voice sounded relaxed. Lepic called back, "Gladly would we join you, friends. But now we must prepare for a patrol."

Jarrell reached the break in the left wall and turned into it without haste. His men sauntered in after him.

The instant they were all in, Jarrell eased back for a cautious peek into the passageway. The men were still squatting around the fire, no longer looking in Jarrell's direction. Jarrell turned and they moved through the collapsing structure and out of it, into a gloomy, rubble-filled street. They were in the right fortress section now. But time was narrowing in on them, with the right building still to be reached.

They threaded through the ruins as swiftly as they could without attracting attention, not going through any new area without checking it out first. They passed a corral where most of the horses were penned, inside a semi-circle of low walls with two strands of rope tied across the ends. And then, dead ahead of them, was what they had come for: the low, roofless garrison building inside whose walls Venturi had been taken down the hole.

Jarrell crouched with his three-man team in a crumbling doorway and scanned the area around it. Everything was pretty much as it had been when he'd studied it from above in daylight. What he could not see from this angle his memory filled in. The four walls were still solid up to a height of about seven feet. It had one doorway. A guard shrouded in a black hooded burnoose sat on the ground in that doorway, looking out; holding a Belgian-made 9 mm P. B. UZI submachine gun on his crossed legs. The holes that had been windows on each side of the doorway showed nothing but darkness inside the walls. There'd been no men camped in there when Jarrell had looked from above. It was unlikely that there were now; these warrior-bandits preferred their tents.

There were a lot of black tents spread around the area in front of the garrison building; and a lot of armed warriors settled in circles around small fires. Those facing he building had a clear view of its front and two sides.

But not the back wall, which was windowless and partially joined to the dark ruins of another building.

"Gerd," Jarrell whispered, "you've got a full view of it all from here, and this is where we have to come through on our way out. Get back here ready to cover us, if we need covering."

Gerd nodded his handsome head. His eyes were unnaturally bright. It could have been dedication, or merely excitement. Fear was something he longed for but didn't know. He gave Chalker the Schmeisser machine pistol and took the M-16, which was good for either close work or middle-distance shooting. The two of them stayed there and watched Lepic follow Jarrell off at an angle through the ruins. In a moment they had vanished, circling to get behind the garrison building.

Chalker checked his watch.

In the disintegrating ruins behind the blind wall of the garrison building, Jarrell paused in shadow and sheathed his knife. He could feel the adrenalin pumping in him. He moved forward, placing each step carefully and silently. Lepic stayed crouched down behind him, watching and waiting.

Jarrell reached the rear wall and rose up on his toes. Reaching up, he investigated the top of the wall with his fingertips, gently removing loose stones and pieces of clay. Then he hooked both hands on the wall top, and slowly chinned himself upward until his eyes were just above the wall.

He could see nothing from there but the top of the other three walls, and the black tops of the tents out front. Which meant, Jarrell hoped, that no one out there could spot him, in turn. Carefully bringing one leg up to one side, he swung his body just enough to hook his ankle on the wall top. He hung that way for a second, then quietly swung the rest of him over on top of the wall, stretching out flat along it.

For a moment he didn't move, just listened and looked. There was no sound of alarm. He didn't see anyone looking his way. The big dark room below him was empty. In the middle was the hole in the ground, and stone steps leading downwyard, faintly illuminated by a dim lamp somewhere far below.

The guard still sat in the doorway, his back to Jarrell, gazing out at the tent encampment.

He moved very slowly, hands hooked on the wall top as he lowered himself down inside the building. His arms ached with the strain of the slowness. His toes touched the ground at last, felt around to make sure there was nothing loose or breakable under them before letting his heels come down to help sustain his weight. All the time, Jarrell kept his head turned, watching the back of the guard sitting in the doorway.

The head didn't turn. Jarrell let go of the wall and lowered his arms, feeling the blood surging through his veins again. He turned fully, cautiously, until his back was to the rear wall and he was facing the back of the guard in the doorway. With infinite caution, he moved sideways to the left wall, crouched, and moved in its darkness under the side window to the front wall, along that and under the window there. Now he was between the window and the doorway. The guard hadn't stirred; hearing nothing to alert him. Jarrell stayed there, pressed against the wall. He looked at the top of the rear wall. Mahjoub Lepic was on it, stretched out flat.

Jarrell returned his attention to the back of the guard sitting in the doorway, less than two feet from him.

SIXTEEN

Two figures in hooded burnooses, in no way different from most of the guerrillas encamped among the fortress ruins, strolled between the black tents and the garrison building. They turned from the tents and approached the guard in the doorway. The warriors among the tents watched them, idly. They assumed that Chalker and Gerd were friends going to exchange a few words with the guard. Everyone knew the guard wouldn't let even friends pass inside, without Ben Hafidi's express permission.

The guard looked up at them curiously as they approached. He couldn't make out their shadowed faces inside the hoods; didn't recognize them by build or manner of walking. By the time they stopped side by side in front of him, and he could see their faces, their long robes hid him completely from any other watching eyes.

Those who watched from the tents and fires saw the two remain standing there for some time, apparently in deep conversation with the unseen guard in front of them. When the two finally turned away, the guard was visible again; still sitting there in the doorway.

Someone was sitting there—wearing the guard's hooded burnoose and holding the same UZI across his folded legs.

Chalker and Gerd disappeared back inside the ruins that afforded a clear view of the garrison building and tents. Gerd took up his position there inside the ruined doorway, with the M-16 held ready. Chalker, the Schmeisser hung on his shoulder, circled away toward the rear of the garrison building.

Inside it, Jarrell was crouched between the hole in the ground and the stripped body of the guard, beside which lay Lepic's repeating shotgun. He reached inside his robes and drew out his handgun, the Walther P-38. It had a silencer screwed into it now. Jarrell snicked off the safety as he looked at the back of Lepic, sitting there in the doorway.

If someone wanted to exchange pleasantries in passing, Lepic could pull it off. If somebody who knew the guard came over for a real talk, all hell would instantly break loose.

There was a faint sound. Jarrell looked up the rear wall. Chalker was stretched along the top. Holding the P-38 in one hand, Jarrell scooped Lepic's discarded burnoose off the ground with the other and started down the stone steps into the hole.

He held the gun down against the folds of his own burnoose as he went down, so it wouldn't be immediately noticeable. At the bottom of the first flight of steps was a corridor, a lamp, and an armed guard lounging on a stool against the wall. The guard saw a burnoosed figure coming toward him; and saw nothing to be disturbed about. He asked a question, but there was no alarm in his voice. He began to frown when the figure continued advancing without an answer. Then he saw the face inside the hood, and it was too late for him.

He had a revolver lying on his lap and a rifle leaning against the wall beside him. He started to reach for both at the same time and Jarrell shot him twice in the heart at a range of three inches. The silencer made whispering sounds of the shots, and Lepic's wadded burnoose jammed across the guard's face stifled his death cry. There was nothing that would carry through the thick surrounding stone—up or down. His body jerked off the stool and Jarrell's gun arm whipped around him, lowering the limp body quietly to the stone floor.

Jarrell took the time required to strip the hooded burnoose from the dead man; a matter of seconds. Twisting it with Lepic's around his left hand, he moved through the corridor with the P-38 leading the way. There was another stone stairway, with no light showing at the bottom of it. Jarrell groped down soundlessly, followed a second passage in darkness by the feel of one wall against his shoulder.

Another flight of stone steps led further into the bowels of the rock under the ruins. There was a glimmer of lantern light down there. Jarrell went down most of these steps in slow silence. The last ten steps he covered on the jump, face and gun looking toward the source of the light.

A guard sat under a lantern against a thick door, with a submachine gun on his thighs. Jarrell squeezed the trigger three times, very fast, as he ran at him. The bullets nailed the guard to the door. He gave a thin scream of pain that had no chance of carrying all the way up through the stone and out into the open, then rolled away from the door and sprawled out across his submachine gun. Jarrell stepped over him and yanked back the bolts locking the door, then instantly turned and crouched to begin stripping away the burnoose from the body.

Marcel Venturi came out of the cell followed by Diana and Michele, hands shielding their slitted eyes from the sudden light.

"I *told* these ladies you were dependable," Venturi said, without any intended humor.

Jarrell threw one burnoose at him, and rose to help the women get into the other two. They helped as much as they could with their eyes still adjusting; too frightened to speak, knowing their lives depended on instant obedience.

Venturi had his burnoose on and the hood around his head while they were still at it. He bent and dragged the submachine gun from under the dead body, set it for automatic fire, and made a low growl of pleasure.

"We move fast now," Jarrell told the two women. "Very fast. Stay with me, right behind me unless I tell you otherwise, and we'll have you out of here."

"Marcel told us," Michele said shakily. "He said—"

Jarrell wasn't listening. He was already moving past Venturi, sprinting up the stone steps. They raced after him.

He got to the top, to the hole leading out into the open, and motioned for them to stay still below him. Then he raised his head and looked out. Lepic was still sitting in the doorway; Chalker was still stretched atop the rear wall.

Jarrell put away the P-38 and unslung the AR as he went up out of the hole. Venturi came up after him, saw the repeating shotgun on the ground and snatched it up, slinging the submachine gun on his shoulder. Jarrell, crouched, pointed at the rear wall as Diana and Michele came up. Chalker reached down one hand as they hurried to it. He pulled Diana up first, as easily as if she weighed nothing at all, and deposited her out of sight down behind the wall. Then he did the same for Michele, and vanished himself.

Jarrell hissed at Lepic as Venturi went up over the rear wall. Then he followed.

Lepic stood up in the doorway and stretched sleepily. He turned and strolled inside the building, and was swallowed by its interior darkness. Those watching from the tent encampment could assume he'd gone in to have some water he'd left there. But they wouldn't go on assuming that, when he didn't come back out. He went over the back wall with the UZI hung on his back, and dropped down with Jarrell and the others.

Jarrell circled away swiftly through the ruins, leading Venturi, Michele, Chalker, and Diana. Lepic brought up the rear, unslinging the UZI and looking back. Still no yells from anyone going to find out why there was no guard in the doorway any more.

They reached Gerd. Still no alarm. Still no need for covering fire to protect their exit. But Gerd stayed in position, watching the area of the black tents, until all the others were past him following Jarrell. Then he turned and went after them.

Jarrell, Lepic, and Venturi moved through the ruins in the lead, the two women close behind them, then

Chalker and Gerd guarding the rear. They went out of one ruined building and across a starlit open space toward another. They were about to enter when Bel Zaara came out of it, with Omrani and another former army officer. They all stopped dead, facing each other.

Bel Zaara might not have recognized Jarrell from a few years back. But he had no trouble recognizing that two of the hooded figures were Michele and Diana.

He opened his mouth and Jarrell took a fast step forward and kicked him in the stomach. Bel Zaara collapsed as though broken in half. The intended yell came out of his open mouth a low choking noise. He hit the ground on his knees, bent double with his fingers clawing feebly at his broken middle. Jarrell kicked him in the head, the boot heel slamming into his temple. As hard as he could. There was no time for fine judgments.

Bel Zaara's head snapped around over his shoulder. He sagged sideways, twitched several times, and then lay still with his neck twisted at an unnatural angle.

Colonel Omrani and the junior officer were frozen in place, looking into the guns aimed at them and keeping their mouths very shut. Omrani didn't even move when he saw Venturi shift his grip on the shotgun, hefting it like a club. He only shut his eyes tightly in the split second before the shotgun's barrel clouted him across the ear and dropped him in an unconscious sprawl. The junior officer whispered, "Please . . ." And was clubbed to a limp sprawl across Omrani.

Chalker and Gerd had already twisted to cover the area behind them, their weapons up in firing position. Jarrell looked left and right, saw no one, and motioned to Lepic. They darted into the building the three had come from, twisting their backs to each other with the first step inside, Jarrell swinging the AR in one direction and Lepic covering the other direction with the UZI.

No one else was in there. The sounds in the surrounding ruins remained normal. Nothing barred their way. Jarrell motioned the others in and headed through in the direction of the tunnel to the outer fortress ruins. Luck was still with them.

And then it wasn't.

There was a shrill yell back behind them, from the direction of the garrison building. Someone had wondered enough about why there was no longer a guard in the doorway to find him dead inside. The yelling was taken up by others, spreading through the ruins. Their time had run out. All around them the sounds ceased being normal and became the noises of warriors springing into movement.

Jarrell sprinted out of the building and dodged away toward the horse corral, drawing his knife as he ran. The others ran past him in the direction of the tunnel, Lepic leading Michele and Diana, Chalker on one side of them and Venturi on the other, Gerd running behind them but half-turned to watch the rear.

There were no precisely laid-out tactics to be stuck with now; and no time for any of them to wait for Jarrell's orders before each move. From now on everything depended on what came at them in any moment; and on whether Jarrell had picked the right men. Each man was his own general, ruled only by the general objective of getting out; using common sense and experience to coordinate properly with the actions of the others.

Jarrell slashed the two ropes stretched across the corral opening, and charged after the others. A hooded warrior appeared beside the corral wall behind him, going down on one knee to aim a rifle at Jarrell's back. Gerd twisted slightly and the M-16 jerked in his hands, firing a two-shot burst that kicked the warrior off his knee and dropped him in an inert sprawl against the corral wall. Jarrell called after Venturi, who spun and fired the shotgun into the corral. At that distance the load of shot spread too wide to do the horses any real damage. But it stung them into frightened motion.

Venturi fired in another load and the horses charged out of the corral, screaming in panic. Jarrell yanked a grenade from his waist rope. It was hung by its firing ring. Detaching the grenade automatically primed it. He counted, twisted, and lobbed it upward. It exploded in the air above the charging horses, scattering them in terror through the ruins in different directions. Adding to the confusion and making them that much harder to catch and mount.

Jarrell and Chalker sprinted up on either side of Lepic as he reached the passageway leading to the tunnel through the joined defense walls. They went past him into it on the jump, splitting left and right.

Dark figures crossing the fire-lit end of the passageway stopped and spun to fire. Jarrell's finger closed on the trigger as he jerked the AR left, right, and left again, the weapon jolting in his hands as it spat sweeping flails of steel-jacketed bullets that lashed the figures and dropped them like broken puppets.

Chalker was charging into the tunnel, yanking a grenade and flinging it through ahead of him without wasting the time to check whether anyone was on the other side. He flung himself flat inside the tunnel; then sprang back up off the ground after the grenade exploded. He charged the rest of the way through. Two guerrillas sprawled there, shredded by the exploding schrapnel.

Jarrell went through the tunnel after him with the others, ramming a fresh magazine into his AR, automatically noting others using the brief lull to reload weapons. Gerd came last, backing through the tunnel and watching the rear. A shadow shifted between ruined walls back there. Gerd let go a precise three-shot burst that hammered the shadow away into deeper darkness.

Reaching the harem courtyard of the outer fortress, Jarrell and Chalker split apart in the lead as a scouting team, searching the way ahead and to either side. Venturi strode after them, holding the shotgun ready in one hand and the wrist of Rosen's daughter with his other. Lepic came close behind with the UZI and Michele Bishop. Gerd stayed with the rear-guard position, half-backing after them, scanning the shadows behind.

The harem area was quiet and empty. The main center of enemy sounds was back in the inner fortress, where warriors were combing the ruins for them in search parties, while others tried to catch stampeding horses. But there was a growing area of activity in the other direction, ahead of them. Around the way out of the ruins to the canyon. Men were being called in to seal off the exit there. They mustn't be allowed the time to complete the sealing off.

Jarrell snapped soft orders and vanished off to the left. Chalker circled right and disappeared. Gerd, Venturi, and Lepic formed into a protective wedge around Michele and Diana, angling fast toward the way out to the canyon. They reached the end of a group of ruins and paused to look beyond, at the crumbling gateway in the outer defense wall, and the canyon beyond that.

Between them and the way out were the cluster of black tents; and too many armed warriors. Eight of them were already in the gateway, completely blocking it. About fifteen more were streaming out of the ruins from various directions to join them.

There was an explosion inside the ruins to the right. Then another, followed by a wild scream. And then a third explosion. That had been Chalker who'd screamed, lending realism to the detonations of the grenades he was dropping behind him as he circled in there at a run.

The warriors heading for the gateway stopped, turned, and charged into the ruins where the explosions had sounded. But the eight already in the gateway stayed there, their automatic rifles held ready as they watched the others vanish among the collapsed buildings.

Jarrell came into view, sprinting along the top of the outer defense wall toward the gateway opening. The submachine gun was slung on his shoulder and each hand brought up a live grenade as he ran. The eight down in the gateway were looking in the wrong direction and didn't see him coming. But then they heard his pounding steps, and some whirled to look up.

By then Jarrell was above the gateway. He dropped both grenades into it and threw himself flat on top of the wall, hugging it with his head down. Three of the warriors in the gateway reacted quickly enough to leap away and fling themselves to the ground before the grenades went off. The other five weren't fast enough. The double thuds of the detonations were cut through by the screams of the dying and groaning of the helplessly wounded.

The three who'd escaped the blasts rose up off the ground. Gerd charged straight for the gateway, mowing them down with precise short bursts from the M-16. Lepic ran after him with Diana and Michele. Venturi, following them, saw six warriors who'd managed to get mounted ride out of the ruins on his left.

He twisted and poured three loads of shot into them; pumping and firing and pumping again, as fast as he could. The stung horses plunged madly, crashing into each other, throwing riders, racing back into the ruins. Only two riders managed to keep control of their horses. Jarrell's AR stammered from the top of the defense wall, hammering them off their mounts.

Venturi sped on through the gateway. Lepic was drawing Michele with him into the canyon. Venturi caught up to Diana, seized her hand, and took her into the canyon after them. Gerd had turned in the gateway and was reloading with his back pressed to one wall. Two unhorsed riders stretched out on the ground and fired at him, the slugs chopping clay dust out of the wall on both sides of him. Jarrell's AR lashed the rest of its magazine at them from the top of the wall, flopping one over on his back with his chest caved in and sending the other fleeing into the ruins without his gun.

Chalker dashed out of the ruins, firing behind him with the Schmeisser. Figures appeared at the edge of the ruins on either side as the Schmeisser went empty. Gerd began cutting them down with fast, spaced bursts as Chalker sprinted the rest of the way.

Jarrell jumped down the other side of the wall, beside the open gateway. Chalker came through it running as fast as he could, and kept on going.

Jarrell shouted: "Gerd!"

Gerd twisted out of the gateway to him, and they sprinted after Chalker into the canyon.

The others were already out of sight beyond the other end of the canyon bend. Jarrell, Chalker, and Gerd ran through it and around the bend, and saw the others running far ahead of them toward the canyon mouth: Venturi with Rosen's daughter, Lepic with Michele Bishop.

Santiso Josal was halfway down the straight stretch in the middle of the canyon. He stood holding a cigarette lighter in one hand. In his other were the ends of two fuses that ran towards opposite walls. He waited until Chalker went past him, then Jarrell and Gerd. Then he thumbed the lighter and lit one fuse, dropped it and started to light the other.

A light gust of wind blew out the flame of the lighter. He thumbed it frantically, and it didn't light; thumbed it again with still no result. The other fuse was burning swiftly away toward the dynamite planted in the canyon wall on his left.

The lighter caught on the third attempt. Josal lit the other fuse, dropped it and the lighter, and sprinted after Jarrell and Gerd. He'd taken three long, driving strides when the whole left wall of the canyon behind him blew outward with a thunder whose shock waves knocked him off his feet.

Josal rolled on the ground, came to a dazed stop, and desperately scrambled back to his feet. A slab of stone the size of a truck came down on top of him.

Jarrell, looking back as he ran away, saw it happen. Saw, too, the tons of shattered rocks that crashed down on top of the place where Josal had been wiped out, as the left wall kept breaking away and falling. He kept running. The other wall would go any second.

When it went, the ground jumped wildly under Jarrell's feet. He stumbled and went down on one knee, his ears stuffed with the shock of the explosion. A huge boulder bounced past him and came to a stop ten yards behind the fleeing Gerd. Jarrell lurched to his feet and pushed on, with the canyon walls still thundering down behind him.

He got to the others, waiting for him inside the canyon mouth. They were all there. All except Santiso Josal. Nora Devlin was coming down from her hiding place dragging the pack containing the radio. Lepic met her and took the pack, slung it on his back, and got his arms through the canvas loops. Gerd was getting the Lee-Enfield and Garand from behind the rock where they'd left them.

He tossed the Garand to Jarrell, who caught it one-handed, holding the AR ready in his other hand.

"Josal?" Venturi asked.

"He bought it," Jarrell told him shortly, and turned to look back down the canyon.

The walls had stopped falling. A huge mound of rocks completely blocked the middle of the canyon. Ben Hafidi's warriors could climb over that to pursue them; but they'd never be able to bring their horses over with them. It would be men on foot after people on foot. With the rest of the night in which to lose the pursuers.

"Move out," Jarrell said, and turned back to lead the way.

And stopped.

A group of mounted warriors were riding into the shadowed canyon mouth from the night darkness outside.

"Scatter!" Jarrell yelled, and leaped for the protection of a boulder, firing the AR one-handed at the riders coming in through the murk.

The one thing that could still stop them had happened: One of Ben Hafidi's roving patrols chancing to come in while they were still there.

Jarrell estimated about fifteen of them as he fired and heard others firing; saw two riders fall in the first ragged barrage. Venturi was down behind a rock to Jarrell's left, his shotgun pumping load after load into the horses; driving them mad with the stinging pains, causing them to rear and plunge, throwing riders, ramming into each other as they whirled to get out of the canyon mouth.

By the time the last of the horses were gone, many of the warriors were dismounted and down behind cover just outside the canyon mouth, starting to fire back blindly.

"Hold your fire unless you see something to shoot at!" Jarrell called to his men, and started to turn for a look back into the canyon.

Bullets sang past his unprotected back and rang off rocks. As he'd feared, the warriors from inside the ruins were beginning to reach the top of the high rock barricade in the middle of the canyon.

185

"Against the base of the wall!" Jarrell shouted, and started to shift position.

Marcel Venturi shifted ahead of him, going on the jump from his rock toward the cliff. Something struck him in midjump, flinging him completely around and dropping him on his back. Jarrell got to him with two long strides, bent to drag him to safety. He froze bending over Venturi, staring. "Marcel—"

Venturi's chest was dark, shiny pulp. His wide-open eyes stared unseeingly at the stars above the canyon.

Something inside Jarrell stopped working. One part of him knew he had to jump over Venturi's body and dive to cover. But another part refused, holding him there over Marcel Venturi's dead face, not letting him move.

Bullets whipped past him, chopping up dirt, spanging off rocks. One of them bounced back and ripped across Marcel Venturi's dead face.

Jarrell came part way out of the trance, abruptly. But not to dive for cover. He went berserk, twisting around in plain sight, dropped the Garand, and raised the AR in both hands, firing a long sweeping burst that lashed back and forth along the top of the rocks choking the middle of the canyon. The uninterrupted flail of lead swept two figures off the top, and sent others ducking back down to cover behind the rock barricade. The AR went empty. Jarrell continued to stand there, squeezing the trigger.

"Jarrell! Get down, dammit!"

He turned his head numbly and stared. Nora Devlin stood in the open, with the revolver she'd finally accepted raised in both hands, firing shot after shot at the middle of the canyon. The shots hit nothing but rocks, but momentarily kept the snipers down out of sight behind them. Gerd's rifle and Lepic's submachine gun joined in.

Nora's gun clicked on an empty. She didn't realize it, with the hammering of gunfire around her. She squeezed the trigger twice more, standing in the open and yelling again: "Jarrell, damn you!"

A bullet kicked up a shower of dirt beside her feet.

Jarrell broke from the paralysis then, diving at her with his arms spread wide. His shoulder caught her across

186

the thighs and dumped her to the ground with him. His arms closed around her tightly and he did a fast roll behind a boulder as slugs chopped splinters off the top of it.

For a moment he just lay there, holding her. His face was a cold mask, but his eyes were no longer dead. There was thinking behind them again. Jarrell got his knees under him and worked deeper into the protection of the boulders at the base of the canyon wall, where the others were barricaded. Lepic had Michele and Diana down flat on the ground there. Gerd and Chalker leaned against boulders, snapping off occasional shots to keep the enemy away in both directions.

"They have us trapped between them," Lepic growled as Jarrell shoved Nora down beside him. "No way out. They'll wait until daylight and——"

"There's a way out," Jarrell cut in flatly. His voice was steady and just loud enough for them all to hear. "Up over one of the caved-in sections of canyon wall back there."

Chalker laughed softly and without humor, not turning from his study of the inner canyon. "They've got one fucking helluva lot of men down below there, that might not let us just climb past."

"They won't stay there," Jarrell said, quietly. *"We're* going out the front way. You, me, Gerd. They aren't sure how many we are, and they won't be able to see how many of us are going out, in the dark." Jarrell looked at Lepic. "You stay here. With the women. And the radio. Until we've drawn them out after us. Wait till they all go out. They will. Then get back through there, and up out of the canyon. Get to those caves you told me about, and through them. There won't be anybody after you if you just keep going. When you're down off the mountains, all you have to do is radio that chopper waiting in the oasis the other side of the border. It'll pick you up and get you out to the Spanish Sahara."

Nora was staring at him. "What about you? And Gerd, and Chalker?"

"We'll make it another way. Without the rest of you

187

slowing us, we can outstalk them and outrun them; with the night to help."

Lepic said nothing. Neither did Gerd or Chalker.

Jarrell looked at Lepic again. "If we make it," he said evenly, "we'll be coming out to that same oasis where the chopper's waiting now. But it'll take time."

"Yes," Lepic agreed tonelessly. "It will take time."

Jarrell had put a fresh magazine in his AR as he spoke. Now he reloaded the Walther P-38 and stuck it in his belt, rising from the ground in a crouch. "Chalker— Gerd—"

They turned from their boulders, nodding; ready to go. Chalker's expression was grim. Gerd's was pleasant, dreamy. Jarrell's was taut, almost eager as he glanced to Nora.

"See you, kid." He dodged out of the boulders, scooping up the dropped Garand as he headed out of the dark canyon mouth. Gerd and Chalker went out after him.

Shots began to snap at them from two sides, but they were running crouched and well apart through the deepest shadows, hard to hit. They didn't shoot back until they were out of sight beyond the canyon mouth. Then the gunfire became intense.

Lepic lay hidden inside the boulders with the three women, listening to it intently. It slackened, then died out entirely. When it resumed a minute later, it was spasmodic firing, much further away from the canyon; and quickly getting even further. Lepic eased forward a bit, until he could see into the canyon.

A single warrior came running into the canyon mouth. He ran past. Warriors began coming over the top of the rock barricade in the middle, climbing down to meet him. There was a hurried conference. Warriors began running through the canyon, out through the entrance. Lepic held himself very still. More and more of them went past; vanishing into the night outside the canyon to hunt down Jarrell, Chalker, and Gerd.

The last of the guerrillas went out to join in the hunt. There were occasional single shots now—far away. The canyon was empty.

Lepic got to his feet and adjusted the weight of the radio on his back. "You heard the man. Let's go."

Nora studied his face as she stood up. *"Do* they have a chance of making it?"

He didn't look away. "If it can be done—if *anyone* can do it, it would be those three men."

SEVENTEEN

It was a very small oasis; just south of the border inside Spanish Sahara. Seventeen palm trees—Nora had counted them a number of times—clustered around a pool of green-blue water that welled up out of some underground stream at this point. All around it, as far as the eye could see, there was nothing but sand, flowing to the horizons.

In the middle of all that desert of sand there was only one landmark of any permanence at all: the pool of water, the palm trees, a helicopter, and three people.

Nora Devlin sat on the sandy ground against a palm, watching the north. There was nothing out there to mark the line on the map where the Spanish Sahara ended and Morocco began. Nothing but yellow sand, yellow sky, and shimmering heat haze reaching to the distant point where sand and sky met.

Mahjoub Lepic sat against another palm near her, gazing at nothing, seeming always half asleep.

Behind them, the helicopter pilot sat on a folding canvas chair pouring the last few drops from a bottle into a paper cup. He drank it, savored it, and looked disgustedly at the empty bottle. "All out of bourbon. I'll tell you what, Miss Devlin: I'm willing to switch if you'll break out that scotch bottle you've got in my chopper."

Nora said: "No." Flat and final.

The pilot sighed. "Look, all this is getting pretty pointless, ain't it? It's eight days since I ferried Bishop's wife and stepdaughter out of here. If those guys haven't come

190

out in eight days, they ain't *gonna* come out."

"*You* can go," Nora told him thinly. "I'm waiting."

The pilot's laugh was harsh. "You kidding? Simon Bishop told me to stick as long as you do. I leave you, and he'll not only fire me, but blacklist me so I can't get another civilian job. And if I went back in the army, he'd probably reach in there and louse me up, too."

"That's your problem." Nora glanced to Mahjoub Lepic. "You don't have to wait with me, either, you know. I never got the impression any of them were that close to you."

"They are not," Lepic agreed simply. "I stay merely out of curiosity. I made a bet with myself; about Jarrell's chances of getting them out alive."

The pilot gave him an interested look. "How do *you* figure the odds?"

Lepic shrugged slowly. "Eight days— It is a very long time."

"Right." The pilot looked at Nora again, altering his tone: "Maybe I sounded hardhearted. I'm not. *I've* lost plenty that were close to me, and I know it hurts. But one thing I sure learned, there's nothing you can do about it. What's done is done."

" 'Leave the dead,' " Nora said, half to herself.

Lepic gave her a curious look.

"Something Jarrell once said," she told him.

He went on studying her, his expression becoming sardonic. "And is one of them so close to *you* that you wait? *I* never got that impression."

"I don't know," she said dully. "I'd just like the chance to find out." She lit a cigarette, took one drag, and stabbed it out in the sand beside her leg.

The sun was close to setting now, turning clouds a gleaming pink with a dark red glow around the edges. The light refracting down from them through the heat shimmer created mirages in the distances. One looked like a large ocean liner, suspended in the air. Another was a group of dark-cloaked riders coming across the sands on camels. Shifts in the refracted light kept changing the mirages. The ocean liner turned upside down, and then lay on its side. Sometimes the approaching camel riders looked like a dozen, at other times they shrank to one or two. The sun sank lower and the ocean liner shriveled away.

The riders were still there, light glinting off their weapons as they seemed to come closer.

The pilot got off his chair, squinting at them. "That's *real*," he decided finally. "Bedouins. With guns." He glanced anxiously to Lepic. "Friendly or trouble, what'd you think?"

Lepic didn't answer for a time. Then he said: "Friendly." He got a cigar from his robes, bit off the end, and lit it.

Nora had never seen him smoke before. She looked from his inscrutable face to the nearing riders.

There were three of them.

Nora stood up and took a step forward to meet them. Then she stopped, turned, and ran to the helicopter.

They rode into the shade under the palms and slid down stiffly and wearily from the camels, looking at Lepic in silence. He gazed back with no words.

Chalker was the first into the water. He hurled himself in, splashing and drinking. Gerd went in next, delicately, swimming across the pool and then back to the middle; floating there and soaking his heat-blistered skin.

Jarrell looked at Nora coming from the helicopter. She had a full bottle of scotch in one hand.

"This has been waiting for you," she said simply, holding it out.

He looked at the bottle, and then at her face. His eyes were holes in a thick mask of caked dust and salt. They stayed on her face for some time.

"If you don't mind," he told her in a voice that rasped, "this time I'll take the liquor after the chaser." He walked into the pool under the palm trees, letting himself fall face down in it, submerging.

It was half a minute before he came up; sitting up to his chest in the water and cupping handfuls against his face.

Nora sat down at the edge of the pool, holding the bottle between her knees and watching him.